'Pede Attack!

With Hunter and Prince Lumen on their backs, Shadow and Ebony, their spiders, jumped into the air, twisted midleap, and landed upside down, clinging to the ceiling of the chamber. The spiders shot capture webs down at the Centipedians, ensnaring dozens.

"Hunter, look out!" Shadow cried out in mind talk.

Hunter ducked just as an Insector spear hurtled past his face. "Thanks," he told Shadow.

"Pay attention!" the spider replied. "The middle of a fight is no time for gathering cobwebs!"

Hunter nodded. Then he shouted, "Battle lance!" His manacle glowed, and the fearsome weapon materialized in his hand.

But the spiders' leap to the ceiling had slowed the Insector attack only slightly. Now the Centipedians were clambering up the walls toward Hunter and the prince.

Lumen batted aside a spear with his sword and gazed down into the pit below them. "I see it!" he said.

Hunter looked down, too, and saw a red gleam of light. They'd found the shard!

Then a mighty blast shook the chamber.

Other Books in the Spider Riders Series

Spider Riders Book One: The Shards of the Oracle

Book Two
Quest of the Earthen

by Tedd Anasti and
Patsy Cameron-Anasti

with Stephen D. Sullivan

A Cookie Jar Entertainment Book

Newmarket Press • New York

Acknowledgments

Grateful acknowledgment is made to the following for their assistance in the preparation of this book: Tedd Anasti and Patsy Cameron-Anasti for creating the world of the Spider Riders; project editor Anne Greenberg for overseeing all of the details; Stephen D. Sullivan for his writing expertise; and, especially, Toper Taylor, whose inspiration and leadership made this book possible, along with his dedicated staff contributors at Cookie Jar Entertainment: Mike Wrenn, Kelly Elwood, and Fonda Snyder.

This book is published in the United States of America.

First Edition

ISBN 1-55704-681-6 (paperback)

10 9 8 7 6 5 4 3 2 1

Library of Congress Cataloging-in-Publication Data

Anasti, Tedd.
  Spider riders : quest of the earthen / by Tedd Anasti and Patsy Cameron-Anasti, with Stephen D. Sullivan.
      p. cm.
  "A Cookie Jar Entertainment Book."
  Summary: Hunter Steele continues his adventures in Arachnia, an underground world with fierce warriors that ride huge, telepathic spiders.
  ISBN 1-55704-681-6 (pbk. : alk. paper)
  [1. Spiders—Fiction. 2. Fantasy.] I. Cameron-Anasti, Patsy. II. Sullivan, Stephen D. III. Title.
PZ7.A5186Spi 2005
  [Fic]—dc22   2005033979

QUANTITY PURCHASES

Companies, professional groups, clubs, and other organizations may qualify for special terms when ordering quantities of this title. For information, write Special Sales Department, Newmarket Press, 18 East 48th Street, New York, NY 10017; call (212) 832-3575; fax (212) 832-3629; or e-mail info@newmarketpress.com.

www.newmarketpress.com

Manufactured in the United States of America.

We, Tedd and Patsy, dedicate this book to each other.

CONTENTS

QUEST OF THE EARTHEN

BOOK TWO

1
Tangled Webs

Darkness pressed in around Hunter Steele. He felt hot and uncomfortable, though the chamber's air remained cool and dry. A bead of sweat fell from a lock of his red hair and ran down his forehead to the bridge of his nose. Hunter smeared away the rivulet with the back of his hand and took a deep breath.

He glanced warily at the stone figures lining the sides of the huge, vaulted room. Each statue depicted a gallant Spider Rider warrior dressed in full battle armor. Each statue rested on a granite sarcophagus—an ornate coffin for the hero carved above. Gigantic images of spiders were carved into the room's walls. For all Hunter knew, the walls were real Turandot spiders that had been turned to stone. A shudder ran down his spine.

"This place gives me the creeps," Hunter said.

His companion, the Turandot girl Corona, frowned at him. "This is our Hall of Heroes," she said as they made their way down the length of the room. "It is the most honored cavern in Arachnia."

Hunter shrugged. "I know," he said, "and we've been coming here for weeks, but it *still* gives me the creeps. The place is like a combination museum and graveyard."

Corona looked puzzled—a look the boy from the surface world had grown used to while living among the Spider Riders.

Hunter's face reddened. "I mean…obviously," he said, "it *is* a combination museum and graveyard, but still…"

Corona gave a little sigh as she smiled. "Everything seems to give you 'the creeps,'" she said. "I sometimes wonder why you stay in the Inner World." She arched a playful eyebrow at him.

"As if I have a choice?" Hunter snapped. As he spoke, memories of how he came to this strange, spider-filled world flashed through his mind.

Hiking near his home, Hunter and his friend Dave had found an old mining pit. Dave slipped and fell in. Hunter pulled Dave out but accidentally fell in himself.

The pit turned out to be bottomless, or nearly so. Hunter had slid through vast caverns and tunnels, unable to stop. Finally, he'd tumbled into this place, Arachnia: the world at the earth's core.

Just after his arrival, Corona had rescued Hunter from a giant deadly bug that she called an Insector. Later, Corona and Hunter had become friends—and maybe more.

She was a Spider Rider—a warrior bonded to a ten-foot-tall telepathic spider. Hunter had joined the Spider Riders to battle the Insector menace. He secretly hoped that becoming a Spider Rider might help him get home, to the earth's surface. Now he had to shield such thoughts from the others, even from his own trusted battle spider, Shadow.

All that had flashed through Hunter's mind as he'd said, "As if I have a choice?"

He immediately regretted his harsh tone. Aside from his battle spider, Shadow, Corona was Hunter's closest friend in Arachnia.

He looked at her anxiously, but she seemed to have taken his comment in stride. She shrugged. "Life seldom gives us all the choices we want."

Hunter nodded.

Corona always put up with his bad moods. She seemed to understand the isolation he felt as the only Earthen in the kingdom of the Turandot people and their huge spiders.

Also, she knew as well as he did that the only way Hunter could leave this strange, underground world was to become an Arachna-Master—a great Spider Rider—and Hunter was still a long way from that.

"Do you think Petra will be better today?" Hunter asked, changing the subject.

Corona shook her head. "I don't know," she replied. "The Oracle has more power than when Petra fell in battle, but…"

She walked confidently into the darkness at the far end of the huge chamber. The crystals on the manacle bracelets that she and Hunter each wore shone dimly, providing the only light in the huge room.

Corona halted before a stone bier about three feet high. Atop the platform lay an unmoving figure. This was not one of the vault's statues, though. It was a young woman—a Spider Rider encased in a delicate, almost transparent cocoon. Words carved on the side of the bier read:

Petra

Leader of the Lost Legion

Her sacrifice was not in vain

Hunter stopped beside Corona and bowed his head. He gazed down at Petra. Her skin was pale, her eyes closed. If Hunter hadn't known better, he would have thought she was dead.

"Arachnia can never repay her," Corona said quietly.

Hunter nodded. Corona and Petra had a lot in common: both were Spider Riders, and both would do anything to protect their people. That devotion had nearly cost Petra her life.

"You're right," Hunter said. "All we can do is keep fighting the Insectors until we get all the shards back."

Terrible images of the recent battle against the Centipedian army flashed through Hunter's mind. The city of Arachnia had nearly fallen that day. Only Petra's sacrifice had allowed Hunter to discover a way to defeat their enemies.

"She shouldn't be here," Hunter said quietly.

Corona bristled. "You think she's not worthy?"

"No," Hunter replied, "she's not *dead*. She should be in the hospital, waiting until we can cure her. I mean, we've recovered two more shards since she was injured, but..." He threw up his hands in frustration.

"Petra's cure may come only when the Oracle is fully restored," Corona reminded him. "Until then, this is the safest place for her. Even if the Insectors invaded the city again, they would not find her here."

Corona leaned down and kissed her comrade on the forehead through the white veil of the cocoon. "Sleep well, Petra," she whispered. "We will not fail you."

Hunter did the same.

"I swear we'll cure you, Petra," he said. "I won't rest until we do!"

"I'm glad to hear that," a stern voice said.

Hunter spun and saw Igneous, the captain-general of the Spider Riders, standing in the shadows near the room's entrance. Sleek Spider Rider battle armor adorned Igneous's tall, muscular frame. He stepped out of the darkness, looking somewhat amused at Hunter's surprise. "I thought I might find you two here," the Spider Rider commander said.

"I suppose you've been talking to our spiders behind our backs," Hunter said, a bit more peevishly than he meant to. Turandot spiders shared a telepathic bond with their riders. Hunter's spider, Shadow, or Corona's mount, Venus, could easily have told Igneous where to find them.

Igneous shook his head. "Instinct," he replied, "something you should learn more about, Earthen. Instinct and the fact that you two visit Petra every time you return from patrol."

"I guess that makes us reliable," Hunter said. Every time the two of them talked, Hunter got the feeling that Igneous didn't like him much.

"Reliable is good," Igneous replied. "Predictable is not. Insectors like predictable riders. Be too predictable in the field and, well…" He shrugged and glanced at the cocooned warrior lying nearby. Hunter glowered at him.

Corona stepped between them. "Was there something you wanted, Igneous?" she asked.

The commander smiled at her. "We have a new mission," he replied. "The Oracle has detected the location of another missing shard—the sixth. It's in a Centipedian lair less than two sleeps' ride from here."

The Inner World's sun was the earth's core. Because it was stationary it was always day. There was no sunset, no night as he knew it, so Hunter quickly translated the Turandot term *sleep* into the earth term *day*.

"Recharge your manacles at the Forge, and meet me by the east wall," Igneous continued. "Prince Lumen will be leading the expedition."

"Great," Hunter said, not quite meaning it.

He telepathically relayed the information to Shadow, who was resting in the spider compound outside the castle. Hunter's mind-talk abilities had increased over the past weeks, so contacting his spider partner from this distance was no problem.

"Maybe this will be the shard that cures Petra!" Hunter thought to Shadow.

"Don't get impatient," Shadow thought back. "The Oracle's full powers won't return until all eight crystals are restored to her crown."

Hunter's heart fell for a moment, but then Shadow added, "Venus and Corona think there might be a chance, too." Spiders and their riders frequently shared thoughts, and the spiders often spoke to one another telepathically as well, but they always shielded these personal conversations from the humans.

Hunter turned to Corona and smiled. "C'mon," he said. "Let's go!"

Dungobeet scurried through the fortress of Mantid the Magnificent. Dungo's antennae twitched nervously, and his bug eyes darted everywhere as he walked deeper into the lair of the Insector ruler. The smooth, arching vaults of Mantid's citadel rose steeply around Dungo, making the beetlelike Insector feel small and insignificant—which was exactly what the palace had been designed to do.

Three of Dungobeet's fist-size messenger bugs flew agitated circles around his carapaced head. They buzzed faster as Dungo paused outside the door to the throne room. The beetleoid tried to calm himself for the coming ordeal.

Before he had mastered his nerves, though, the throne room door swung open of its own accord. Dungobeet swallowed hard and stepped inside.

Behind a long, curved marble table sat Mantid's main enforcers—the Big Four Insectors: tall, brutish Stags, the heavily armored warrior; Royal Beerain, beautiful and deadly queen of the hive; cunning, dexterous Grasshop, the inventor; and Buguese, the second in command of the Insector empire. Except for the antennae protruding from his forehead, Buguese appeared nearly human. The Big Four turned their many eyes on Dungobeet. It wasn't they who caused Dungo's legs to shake, though.

Mantid the Magnificent, ruler of the Insector kingdom, watched them all from his raised platform beyond the table.

Mantid was tall, proud, and cruel of countenance. Shining green armor covered his body and insectlike face. A purple satin cloak with gold embroidery adorned his enormous bulk. Two long, scythelike arms protruded from beneath his robes. His vicious eyes focused on the small, quivering Insector standing at the door to his throne room.

Dungobeet scurried into the chamber and knelt on the floor before his master. "I await your instructions, lord," he said, his reedy voice quavering. "Who will protect the remaining shards from the accursed Spider Riders, and how may I help?"

Stags stood and pounded his armored fist on the marble table. "Who will protect them?" he said. "How dare this slime even ask? Beerain and Grasshop have failed—as have all the other weaklings before them."

"We hid the shards as Mantid commanded," Beerain interjected. Her voice buzzed with annoyance.

"You're not blaming the master for choosing defective hiding places, are you, Stags?" Grasshop asked coolly.

"Bah!" the huge beetleoid said. "It's clear that only one of us is worthy to guard the rest of the shards. Only *one* of us has not failed."

"I have not failed," Buguese interjected. The humanlike Insector smiled slightly. "I delivered the shard Mantid gave me to the island of Quagmiro—just as he asked. There it remains, safe and sound."

"Because you do not have the strength to protect it yourself," Stags huffed, "just as Beerain and Grasshop did not have the strength."

"There is more than one kind of strength, brute," Grasshop said.

"You think it's strong to tinker together toys?" Stags asked him.

"Toys that can destroy the walls of Arachnia," Buguese pointed out.

Stags looked as though he might lunge at Buguese. But before he could strike, a blast of searing green energy flashed through the air between them.

"Save your hatred for the Spider Riders," Mantid rasped. He turned to Grasshop. "What progress on our latest weapons?"

"Your subjects in the pits labor admirably, my lord," Grasshop replied confidently. "One lightning thrower is complete. Two more are nearly ready."

Buguese nodded appreciatively. "Three might possibly bring the walls of Arachnia tumbling down," he said. "Despite Centok's defeat, there are more than enough Centipedians remaining to handle the weapons properly."

"With the loss of Centok," Beerain added, "the Centipedians will be more eager than ever to fight—with the right leader." She spoke casually, though it was obvious to all in the room that she was suggesting herself to lead such an expedition.

"Yes," Buguese agreed, "with the *right* leader." He didn't mean Beerain, though—he meant himself.

Dungobeet glanced from one Insector commander to the next. Clearly, all of them relished this job.

Mantid rose. "I think," he said, "that this assignment requires more brute force than finesse. Stags, you will lead the new Centipedian army. I will send the finished weapon with you. Protect the shard that is hidden in the Centipedians' lair, and prepare them to march against the Turandot."

Stags pumped his armored fists in the air. "Yes, my lord. It is my pleasure to serve. I'll hang the Spider Riders from their own webs!"

"It's the spiders who make the webs, not the riders," Beerain pointed out. Stags glared at her.

Mantid ignored their byplay. "Go and prepare, Lord Stags," he said. "And take Dungobeet with you."

2
The Ambitious Princess

Princess Sparkle, dressed in full battle armor, ran out of the palace and across the plaza toward the city wall, where the Spider Riders would be assembling for their new mission. Her spider, Hotarla, lagged slightly behind. In the weeks since Hunter Steele had arrived in the Inner World, Hotarla had grown larger and stronger, but she was still small for a battle spider. Because of her size and her youth, Hotarla had trouble carrying the princess for long periods of time.

"Sparkle, slow down!" Hotarla thought to the princess. "We've been training so hard that I can hardly move!"

"If we slow down, they'll leave us behind—again," Sparkle thought back.

"They'll leave us behind anyway," Hotarla replied. "Lumen didn't call for you to go on this mission."

"We have to show them we're ready," Sparkle said.

"But it could be dangerous," Hotarla warned.

"If you don't want to fight, why have we been working so hard?" Sparkle replied.

"It's every battle spider's responsibility to fight," Hotarla said, "but that doesn't mean we have to fight right now."

The two of them arrived, huffing and puffing at the base of the city wall, just as Prince Lumen, Igneous, Hunter, Corona, the mercenary warrior Magma, and their battle spiders were preparing to leave. They were all so busy securing provisions and checking their equipment that none of them noticed the young princess and her spider.

"Keep tight formation all the way to the lair," Igneous was saying to Hunter. "We don't want them to know we're coming if we can help it."

Hunter frowned at him. "I have been on missions before, you know. We've even recovered shards on a few."

"Don't sass me, Earthen," Igneous replied. "I'd just as soon leave you behind. Your training is still lacking, and you could be a danger to all of us—especially when you don't listen. The prince, though, seems to think you're some kind of good luck charm."

"Igneous," Corona said, "that's not fair. Hunter may not have trained in the usual way, but he's been invaluable to the corps many times."

Now it was Igneous's turn to frown. He started to say something, but the prince interrupted.

"Is everything ready?" Lumen asked.

Igneous nodded a curt bow. "Yes, my prince."

Sparkle saw her chance. She cleared her throat loudly, stepped forward, and said, "We're ready to go, too."

Everyone turned to her, but only Magma smiled. "Hey, webling," he said, "when did you get here? Come to see us off, have you?"

Sparkle crossed her arms over her chest and pouted at him. "No," she said. "I'm here to go on the mission with you."

Because she was a princess, none of the others dared laugh, but through her telepathic connection with Hotarla, Sparkle could tell that they wanted to.

"Sparkle," Lumen said seriously, "you can't come with us. You may wear a manacle now, but you still haven't passed the tests, and—"

"Hunter hasn't passed the tests, either," she interjected. "And Corona just said he'd been invaluable to you many times."

Lumen straightened into a very regal stance and gazed down at his sister. "Sparkle," he said in a fatherly tone that really annoyed the princess, "you are neither old enough nor strong enough to come on missions yet. Someday you will be, but—"

"Hotarla and I have been training," the princess insisted. "We're a lot stronger than we used to be. Take us along with you! We promise we won't let you down."

Magma put his hand on her shoulder. "This job isn't for you, webling," he said. "Give it time. You'll be old enough soon."

Sparkle stared up at the big Spider Rider. She couldn't decide if she wanted to cry or punch him in the face.

"Hunter is sympathetic to us," Hotarla whispered to the princess via mind talk. "I can feel it from Shadow. I don't know if he'll speak up, though."

Sparkle gazed from her brother to Hunter and back. "Hunter thinks I should go," she said.

"No I don't!" Hunter protested. "That's not what I was thinking at all!"

Igneous glared at Hunter, then turned sympathetically toward the princess. "Hunter Steele is not leading this expedition," he said. "Prince Lumen is."

Tears welled at the corners of Sparkle's eyes as she looked at her older brother. "Please?" she pleaded.

Slowly, Lumen shook his head. "I'm sorry," he said. "You're just not ready. Mount up, everyone. It's time to leave."

He and the others climbed onto the backs of their battle spiders and rode up and over the city wall.

Just before they crested the top of the wall, both Magma and Hunter cast sympathetic looks back toward the young princess. Then they turned and rode over the parapet.

Sparkle clenched her armored fists. Tears streamed down her young cheeks.

"We'll show them, won't we, Hotarla!" she said.

Without even waiting for a reply, the princess turned and ran back toward the palace.

Mantid touched a hidden panel in the wall of his throne room. The wall slid open, revealing a smaller, darkened chamber beyond.

In the center of the room a large blob of pale, pulsating gelatinous substance rested on a pedestal several feet high. The pedestal had been fashioned from the exoskeletons of Mantid's defeated enemies. The jumble of armored shapes always brought a smile to the Insector tyrant's cruel face.

Mantid gazed at the quivering mass atop the pedestal. It was a gift from his new ally across the sea in Quagmiro. The jelly glowed slightly as Mantid approached it. The chief Insector paused for a moment, then touched his clawlike hands to the pulsating surface.

"Fungus Brain, are you there?" Mantid said.

In response, the jelly glowed more brightly, and a ghostly form appeared above it. The shape resolved itself into the image of a hideous, misshapen creature. It appeared to be a huge brain with wicked eyes and a drooling gash for a mouth.

Its pale, bloated mass pulsed in time with the jelly atop Mantid's pedestal. Slender tentacles swayed like poised snakes around Fungus Brain as it spoke.

"We are here, O king of the Insectors," the creature's burbling, high-pitched voice replied, "as we promised when we gave you a piece of our essence. We are at your service." The creature's piercing eyes looked directly at Mantid, as though it thought itself the Insector tyrant's equal. "We trust you find this means of communication...convenient?" the blob said.

Mantid returned the thing's gaze. "I find it more convenient, swift, and spyproof than relaying information by Dungobeet's messenger bugs," Mantid replied, "at least in this case." He did not blink as he spoke. "Is the item I sent you safe?"

"The shard lies hidden within our kingdom of Quagmiro, as you requested," Fungus Brain replied. "It will remain there until you call for it."

Mantid nodded. "Good," he said. "Take care, though. The Spider Riders have grown in power. Soon, they will be coming for it."

"We feel the probes of their Oracle already," Fungus Brain replied, "but her telepathy is no match for ours." The hideous visage floating above the pedestal smiled and more drool fell from its flabby lips. "We can keep precise knowledge of the shard's location from them for a while yet."

Mantid nodded. "Until the trap we've planned is ready," he said.

"Of course," Fungus Brain replied, "until our trap is ready, Lord Mantid."

3
A Conference of Spiders

"What was that? Did you hear something?" Hunter asked. He glanced back down the tunnel the way he and the other Spider Riders had come, but he didn't see anything.

Shadow's voice echoed in his head. "I didn't hear anything, and I don't see anything, either. It's probably just nerves."

Hunter found the battle spider's tones reassuring. He and Shadow hadn't been bonded together for very long, but already Hunter could hardly imagine *not* having a giant spider share his thoughts, though he still found it inconvenient at times.

"Ebony wants to know what we're doing," Shadow continued. Ebony was Prince Lumen's battle spider; he and the prince were leading Hunter and the others through a series of disused tunnels at the edge of the Centipedian lair.

"Tell Ebony we're walking along in the dark, just like everybody else," Hunter replied. He'd already grown tired of Ebony and Lumen's constant checking up. Sure, the prince had a lot of responsibility on his shoulders, but it seemed at times as if the prince really didn't trust Hunter to get the job done.

"Lumen's just nervous, too," Shadow assured him. "Don't let it get to you. He's just as young as you are."

"Hey, I'm not *that* young!" Hunter shot back via mind talk.

"Quiet!"

The voice echoing through Hunter's mind now belonged to Venus, Corona's spider. Beneath his armor, Hunter turned slightly red. Usually, spiders mind-talked only to their own riders and to one another. Hunter's mind-talk abilities had grown over the last weeks, as had his ability to conceal stray thoughts. Strong emotions, though, could sometimes accidentally bridge the telepathic gap and broadcast messages to others nearby.

Clearly, Venus, at least, had heard his retort; he hoped she and the other spiders hadn't heard anything more.

"That's all they heard," Shadow assured him. "But be more careful in the future."

"I will be," Hunter thought back.

"What's wrong?" Corona asked as she and Venus pulled up to walk beside Hunter and Shadow.

"Shadow and I were just having a bit of a…debate," Hunter said. He ignored Shadow's telepathic chuckle at the description.

Corona gazed at him, concerned. "You should be more careful," she said.

"Yeah. That's what Shadow said, too," Hunter replied.

A smile flashed across Corona's pretty face. "You know the old saying—'Stray thoughts slay Turandot.'"

"I've heard something like that before," Hunter said. "But I'm from the surface world, remember?"

Corona mimed hitting herself in the head. "How could I forget?" she asked.

Igneous's voice suddenly spoke in Hunter's mind. "You two! Mind-talk only!" he said. Igneous's mind-talk powers almost matched those of Lumen. The captain-general could now talk to both spiders and riders over great distances. "Magma says we're getting close," Igneous concluded.

Magma had once been held captive by this hive of Centipedians. That was why Lumen had chosen the big mercenary to lead this part of the expedition; Magma knew the Centipedian lair far better than anyone else.

Hunter and Corona nodded as the whole squad of agile battle spiders deployed in a flash from the tunnel into a large cavern. Small holes in the ceiling let orangish light from the Inner World sun filter into the chamber.

"Lumen's going to initiate a group mind link," Shadow told Hunter. "That way, we'll be able to coordinate better for the next stage of the plan."

Hunter nodded. He'd heard of this power but had never seen it used before. "Maintaining that kind of telepathic link is a terrible strain, isn't it?" he asked.

"Not as much strain as it is keeping the emotional thoughts of you humans off the link," Shadow replied. "Besides, Lumen's been practicing, and his family is gifted in mind talk."

"Maybe that's why the Arachna family has always ruled the Turandot," Hunter thought back.

"They have since the humans and spiders became allies over a thousand years ago," Shadow said. "Relax now. It will make establishing the link easier."

Hunter nodded again, though the idea of having a lot of people's thoughts running around in his head wasn't very appealing to him. He worried even more about revealing his own deepest thoughts!

As Hunter relaxed, it was suddenly as though someone had put a set of stereo headphones on his head. "This spot is right above the high-security room," Magma's voice said.

"You're sure?" Lumen asked via the link.

"If you didn't trust me," the big rider thought back, "you probably shouldn't have brought me along."

"Brash mercenary!" thought a deep spider voice. "You will speak respectfully to your prince!"

Hunter deduced that the voice belonged to Ebony, Lumen's spider. Several other spider voices hissed their agreement. Each telepathic voice had its own signature. Eventually, Hunter would learn to instantly recognize the telepath by this signature.

"You're not *my* prince particularly," Magma mind-talked. "I'm a mercenary, remember? I'm with you because you pay me."

"Exorbitantly, I might add. But enough banter," Lumen replied. "Hunter, use your sonic charge to dig us a tunnel down to the security room."

"But, my prince," Igneous interjected, "the noise of the Earthen's sonic charge will bring the Centipedians for sure."

"Igneous is right," said a voice that Shadow told Hunter was Igneous's mount, Flame.

Hunter thought it odd to hear the other spiders, as he usually heard only their riders. It was almost like meeting the Turandot spiders all over again. He worked hard to shield this thought so that he wouldn't seem like a complete greenhorn.

"You're learning," Shadow said inside the boy's head.

"I've been training with my sonic charge," Hunter told the others. "By boosting the power use, I can make it almost silent."

"Though that means your manacle will run out of energy more quickly," a kind spider voice said.

Hunter looked at Corona's spider, Venus, knowing the thought must have come from her. He smiled; now that Venus wasn't scolding him, she seemed as gentle and brave as her rider.

"I should have enough power to get us in," he assured the rest. "Just make sure you've got my back."

"That means we need to protect him while he works," Shadow translated.

"Don't we always?" thought a gruff voice. Hunter knew it belonged to Brutus, Magma's spider.

"I trust Hunter's ability," Lumen said. "Let's get started before the Centipedians discover us."

Everyone agreed, and they all formed a protective circle around Hunter as he powered up his sonic charge.

Hunter leaped off Shadow's back. "It'll be quicker if I don't have to dig the hole wide enough for a mounted rider," he explained.

The others in the mind link murmured their agreement.

Hunter concentrated, feeling the energy building around his armored fists. Then he pointed toward the spot in the ground Magma had indicated and whispered, "Sonic charge!"

Waves of nearly silent energy blasted out of his hands, pounding the earth. The shock waves quickly pulverized the ground, sending sprays of dirt and rock into the air. Hunter stepped forward, pushing the invisible force in front of him, digging through the soil. He made the tunnel wide enough for Shadow and the others to follow, one by one.

Lumen had let the group mind-link power lapse, so Hunter followed Shadow's directions, relayed from Magma, as he went.

"Magma says we're very close," Shadow said after they'd gone a hundred yards in. Lumen and Ebony followed right behind, with the rest in line after them.

Hunter glanced at the energy crystal on his manacle. Already it had begun to fade and blink. Just then, part of the wall in front of him collapsed, and he saw a glint of reddish light from beyond.

"The shard!" Hunter thought.

He, Shadow, Lumen, and Ebony, all eager to recover the stolen artifact, pushed through the final feet of dirt. They tumbled into a large chamber octagonal in shape, thirty feet wide, and nearly as high. They'd entered six feet up on one of the walls, near a corner. In the middle of each of the eight walls stood a stone door with a crystal set in its center. The crystals glimmered with pale orange light.

"It's not the shard!" Hunter thought. "It's just some crystals in the chamber doors." He and Lumen turned to glare at Magma, but the big mercenary wasn't there.

"The rest fell behind when we pushed through the final wall," Shadow explained. "Venus says the tunnel ceiling had collapsed a bit, and now they have to clear away the loose rubble before they can catch up."

"We should wait for them," Hunter said.

"Lumen doesn't want to," Shadow relayed. "Brutus told Ebony that Magma found a security vault in the center of this chamber. The Centipedians keep their most precious items there. That's where the shard must be. Lumen wants to find it without delay."

A large, flat capstone six feet wide and two feet thick rested over a well in the center of the chamber. Carvings of Centipedian warriors decorated the stone.

"Can we move it?" Hunter asked silently.

"Ebony and I agree it's too heavy," Shadow replied.

"Hunter," Lumen said via mind talk. "Use your sonic charge."

Hunter looked at the flashing crystals on his manacle. "I'm almost out of power," he said. "I don't know if I have enough energy to do it silently."

"Silence doesn't matter now," Lumen said. His thin face grew stern and determined. "I won't fail when we're so close. We need to get that shard! Hurry!"

Hunter nodded and ear protectors automatically materialized out of the armor that he and Lumen wore. He pointed his manacle at the capstone, and said, "Sonic charge!"

A deafening screech filled the chamber, and the capstone exploded into thousands of tiny fragments, revealing the circular well in the stone floor. Pale red light leaked up from below.

"That's what I'm talking about!" Hunter proudly laughed.

"We've done it!" Lumen cried. "Good work!"

Before his shout echoed away, though, all eight doorways to the room burst open, and a horde of screaming Centipedian warriors rushed in, armed to the mandibles!

4
Light at the End of the Tunnel

The Centipedians swarmed into the chamber, brandishing sawtooth swords and long spears.

Hunter and Lumen drew their stun swords as the Insectors ran forward. Ebony and Shadow fired sleep darts, and four Centipedians fell to the floor, unconscious.

The swarm surged toward them, trying to overwhelm the Spider Riders. Hunter and Lumen slashed at the Centipedians, knocking out five more. The humans remained vastly outnumbered, though.

"We could use some help here!" Hunter shouted, his voice barely audible above the clashing weapons.

"Yes!" Lumen cried with both his voice and mind talk. "Spider Riders, to arms!" His words sounded confident, but when Hunter glanced at him, his eyes looked worried. The mass of savage Insectors surged all around them.

"The others are on their way," Shadow assured Hunter, "but—"

"But what?" Hunter thought back.

Lumen shot an angry look at Hunter. "Ebony says you didn't make the tunnel large enough! Brutus is stuck!"

A telepathic image from the bond he shared with Shadow formed in Hunter's mind. He saw Magma's spider wedged in the tunnel above them—blocking the way.

"It's not your fault," Shadow told Hunter. "Lumen shouldn't have rushed in so quickly."

"Too late for blame games now," Hunter thought back. He turned aside one enemy spear with his sword, but five more stabbed at them.

Both Shadow and Ebony jumped into the air at the same time. They twisted midleap and landed upside down, clinging to the ceiling of the chamber. The spiders shot capture webs down at the Centipedians, ensnaring dozens.

"That buys us some breathing room," Lumen said confidently. "Magma, use your plasma blast to free Brutus!"

Hunter didn't hear Magma reply, though he assumed that Ebony and Brutus must be in mental contact, as the spiders usually were during a battle.

"Hunter, look out!" Shadow cried.

Hunter ducked just in time as an Insector spear hurtled past his face. "Thanks!" he told Shadow.

"Pay attention!" the spider replied. "The middle of a fight is no time for gathering cobwebs!"

Hunter nodded, sheathing his sword. Then he shouted, "Battle lance!" His manacle glowed and the fearsome weapon materialized in his hand. Now that they had gained some distance from the bugs, it would be easier to fend them off with the long spear.

The spiders' leap to the ceiling slowed down the Insector attack only slightly. When they realized what had happened, the Centipedians began clambering up the walls toward Hunter and the prince.

Lumen batted aside a thrown spear with his sword and gazed down into the pit on the floor below them. "I see the shard!" he said.

Hunter looked down, too, and saw a gleam of light at the bottom of a deep, circular stone well. They'd found the sixth shard!

Then a mighty blast shook the chamber, and Hunter nearly lost his grip on Shadow's back.

"Sorry," his spider said, "I should have warned you Magma was about to fire his plasma blast." Shadow leaped forward across the ceiling and down the wall, ramming into five Centipedians rushing toward them. The Insectors lost their footing and fell. The 'pedes landed heavily on the floor of the room and lay there, stunned. Hunter knocked another two off the wall with his lance.

The prince knocked one Insector off the wall with his sword, while Ebony's legs dispatched two more. "We need to get that shard before the 'pedes move it!" Lumen said.

"Igneous, Magma, and Corona should be here in a moment," Hunter reminded him.

"By then it could be too late," Lumen replied. "What if there's another way into that vault that Magma doesn't know about?"

Hunter didn't have an answer for that, so he said, "The pit is too narrow for the spiders. I'll web down and grab the shard while you hold the Centipedians off."

"No!" Lumen barked. Through his mind link with Shadow, Hunter felt the sting of a similar command from Ebony.

"It's my responsibility," the prince said. "You hold back the Centipedians while I rescue the shard."

A momentary flash of anger filled Hunter's mind. It was his plan. Why did Lumen get the glory of rescuing the shard?

"Because he is the prince," Shadow's voice said gently in Hunter's mind.

Hunter silently berated himself for being so hotheaded. He met the prince's eyes and nodded.

Lumen nodded back, though he looked a bit scared. He and Ebony positioned themselves above the pit. Ebony spun a thin, ropelike strand of webbing and shot it down into the passage. Instantly, Prince Lumen slid down the line and into the vault below.

This surprised the Centipedians. Some of them turned and raced back down the wall to try to hack the prince's web line in half.

Just then, the other Spider Riders burst through the tunnel Hunter had carved in the wall.

"What took you so long?" Hunter yelled.

Igneous looked around, worried. "Where's the prince?" he asked.

"In the pit, rescuing the shard," Hunter replied.

Shadow mentally passed the information along to the other spiders. The thoughts traveled at the speed of light, as they always did.

"And you let him?" Igneous said angrily. He glared at Hunter and urged Flame toward the pit to help protect the prince's slender lifeline.

"What was I supposed to do?" Hunter shot back. "He's the prince!"

Hunter and Shadow leaped back down to the floor to help Igneous protect the line. Magma, Corona, and their spiders stayed on the ceiling to keep the Centipedians away from Ebony. The prince's big, black spider had been doing a pretty good job on his own, but he also needed to keep Lumen's web line secure.

Hunter and Shadow landed on top of a group of six Centipedians who were swarming toward the vault pit. Shadow knocked down two with his immense body. He sleep-darted another and felled a fourth like a martial arts expert with a sweep of one hind leg. Hunter knocked the other two over with his lance.

Igneous and Flame fought nearby amid dozens of centipede warriors. The captain-general had managed to keep the Insectors away from the slender web line so far, but with every passing moment, more 'pedes swarmed into the room.

"I suppose it was your idea to let this lot know we were here," Igneous snarled at Hunter.

Although offended, Hunter said nothing and knocked three more 'pedes unconscious with his battle lance.

"Don't think ill of Igneous," Shadow said in Hunter's mind. "He's just worried about the prince."

"Like I'm not?" Hunter thought back. Shadow leaped over three 'pedes and webbed them to the floor while Hunter knocked a thrown spear—aimed at the prince's web line—out of the air.

At the same moment, Lumen grabbed a protruding stone in the wall of the pit to keep his web line from swinging. He gasped in surprise as the stone sank beneath his touch, activating counterweights within the rocky walls. With a heavy grinding sound, a stone security door slid shut just above his head.

The door pinched the prince's web line between itself and the wall of the pit, grinding it against the stones. Lumen knew that a battle spider's web was light but strong as steel. Would it be enough? he wondered. Would it hold?

Lumen touched a symbol on his manacle to activate one of his armor's many devices. A spiderlike contraption crawled out of the bracelet and up his arm, and fitted itself onto his right eye.

Using the device, Lumen scanned the walls. Now he could see within the stone to find out how the security door worked. Forcing himself to remain calm, the prince quickly located the door's hidden release mechanism.

He climbed down a little farther and pushed upward on another handhold—something a climber would normally never do. The rock moved. Counterweights within the walls whirled into motion, and the security door drew back.

The prince let out a relieved sigh. Ebony's web strand had held! Lumen slid down to the shard on the bottom of the pit.

As his armored boots touched the floor, the eyepiece revealed a long horizontal slit in one wall of the pit. Lumen spotted something metal concealed within the wall and dropped to his belly just in time. A knife blade the size of a barn door flashed out like a sideways guillotine. It sliced through the air where, moments before, the prince had been standing.

"Hunter, Corona," Igneous called out on the link, knowing his voice wouldn't be heard above the battle, "push the 'pedes back, and web up the doorways. If these bugs keep swarming in here, we've got no chance."

Hunter and Shadow surged through a dozen seven-foot Centipedians, bowling them over like tenpins. The spider ran at top speed with four of his legs while batting the 'pedes

29

aside with the other four. The boy and his spider reached one door, and Shadow sprayed the doorway with thick, sticky webbing while Hunter protected the spider's back. Like all battle spiders' armor, Shadow's had tiny channels built into it, allowing him to shoot webs from both the back and the front.

Corona and Venus leaped down from the ceiling to one of the doorways next to Hunter and did the same thing.

The two of them moved around the chamber in opposite directions, webbing up the doorways and knocking out every 'pede they encountered along the way.

"Fetch torches! Burn the webs!" one Centipedian cried just before a sleep dart from Venus knocked him out.

"I wondered when they'd think of that," Shadow said.

"Me, too," Hunter mind-talked back. "Let's hope the 'pedes outside the room didn't hear him."

Once the doors had been sealed with webbing, Hunter and the others made quick work of the remaining Centipedians. As Magma punched the last 'pede in the face, Prince Lumen's head appeared above the edge of the pit. The prince looked battered and tired. He grimaced as he pulled himself up the web rope.

"My prince, are you all right?" Igneous asked. He grabbed Lumen's hand and helped him out of the pit.

Lumen nodded. "There were...security traps," he said, "but...I got it." He opened his clenched fist and revealed a glittering shard of the Oracle.

"We've got what we came for," Igneous said. "Move out!"

Instantly, all five spiders and their riders crawled back into the hole Hunter had dug for them. They raced through the tunnel without looking back, Hunter last.

"Hunter," Igneous said, "seal that tunnel behind us."

"Yeah, okay," Hunter said. He glanced at the power crystal on his manacle. It was flickering dimly, an indication that its energy had nearly run out. He figured he had enough left for one good jolt, though.

Turning backward as he rode in his spider surfing stance, Hunter pointed at the ceiling of the tunnel and called, "Sonic charge!"

Waves of sound blasted out of Hunter's manacle and into the hard-packed earth and rock. The structure of the tunnel weakened and then buckled behind them. Tons of earth thundered down, blocking the passageway.

"Good work, Hunter!" Corona called.

The riders bolted out of the tunnel system and across the desert plains. As they did, hundreds of Centipedians swarmed out of hidden entrances to their lair.

The Insectors shot arrows at the retreating Spider Riders, but the spiders were too quick. Before the 'pedes could catch up, Hunter and the others had raced out of range.

Hunter smiled at Corona; she smiled back.

Igneous turned back at them and glared. "Don't be too proud of yourself, Earthen," he said. "Because of you, the prince nearly got himself killed!"

"Before I can even take command, you lose the shard?" Stags bellowed.

He twisted the Centipedian's neck in his powerful claws, and the many-legged Insector fell dead at his feet.

Dungobeet had been about to smile, but the Centipedian's death quickly changed his mind. He looked nervously at Stags, hoping not to be next.

31

Stags rubbed his almost-human chin with one big claw. "If Mantid hears of this," he muttered to himself, "he will blame me."

Dungobeet cleared his throat. "This is a terrible stain on your honor, Lord Stags," the beetleoid said carefully, "but perhaps you could redeem yourself in Mantid's eyes."

"How?" Stags asked.

"By slaying the Spider Riders who took the shard," Dungo suggested.

A glitter grew in Stags's inhuman eyes. "Yeah," he said. "Then I'd be the hero, not the dung pile." He turned and scowled at Dungobeet. "But the ones who took it must be back in Arachnia by now. We'll never catch them."

"They may currently be safe behind their city walls," Dungobeet said, "but they won't be safe forever. In fact, I have a very good idea where they might appear next." His messenger bugs buzzed happily around Dungobeet's head.

"Tell me!" Stags said.

Now Dungo did smile. "Of course, my lord."

5
Fateful Decisions

Hunter, Prince Lumen, and the others gathered in the Sacred Sepulcher, deep within the plateau fortress of the Turandot.

The chamber was huge, with a high, vaulted ceiling held up by pillars that looked like the arching legs of a giant spider.

The statue of the Oracle stood in the center of the room. She was lovely and very human looking—aside from the eight arms that grew from her torso. Three of her arms remained tightly clutched against her chest. The other five, though, were extended to the side, their palms turned upward.

In each palm burned a flickering, almost transparent flame. The flames danced with the colors of the rainbow. The colors were reflected in the five red gemstones set into the elaborate, spiderlike crown atop the Oracle's head.

Three empty spaces remained in the crown, one for each of the three missing shards. Tiny cracks and fissures traced the Oracle's Spider Rider armor; long, flowing skirt; and golden skin—scars from Mantid's evil plot to destroy the statue and her power.

King Arachna stood behind Hunter and the other riders who had rescued the shard. Military matters were left to the young in Arachnia, and the king's only role with the Spider

Riders was to advise his son. The king was a kind-faced, middle-aged man with salt-and-pepper hair. He looked both pleased and proud at the riders' accomplishment. Yet, at the same time, lines of worry creased his forehead. Even with so many of the shards recovered, the kingdom's troubles weighed heavily on him.

Beside him stood Princess Sparkle, who seemed torn between being proud of her brother and annoyed at having not been allowed to go on the mission. She folded her arms across her chest and pouted.

As the king and princess looked on, Prince Lumen approached the Oracle. He held out the newly recovered shard as though he were presenting an offering to the golden statue.

"Great Oracle," he said gravely, "we have bested your enemies again and now return another shard to its rightful place."

He stepped forward and placed the shard into one of the empty sockets in the Oracle's crown. As he did, another of the Oracle's arms unfolded from across her chest. The fingers of that hand slowly opened, and a new, colorful flame sprang from the statue's palm.

Hunter smiled, though he couldn't help wishing that he'd rescued the shard personally.

"You can't be the hero every time!" the distant voice of Shadow echoed in his mind. Hunter pushed the spider's thoughts aside as several cracks on the Oracle's form miraculously mended themselves.

The statue's golden face softened as a pale glow surrounded her. She opened her eyes and looked at the group assembled in the chamber. The flames in the statue's hands grew brighter as she spoke.

"My children," she said, her voice gentle but powerful, "my Spider Riders…thank you. Thank you all. With every shard you recover, more of my powers are restored. But our enemies remain powerful as well. Even now Mantid plots the destruction of our people and our city."

"What else is new?" Magma rumbled. Igneous shot him a stern look.

"Much is new in the world, Magma," the Oracle replied, "much that you cannot see."

Magma turned away, defiant.

"Much that I cannot see, either," the Oracle continued. "The enemy's power grows, even as does my own. He hides his purpose from me—though he cannot completely hide the location of the shards of my being."

"Where are the other shards?" Lumen asked. "Tell us, and we'll recover them!"

"One shard lies in the swamp island of Quagmiro, beyond the Great Sea," the Oracle replied. "Its exact location remains hidden from me. An evil telepathic power works against its discovery."

"And the final shard?" Corona asked. "Do you know where it is?"

"The last shard Mantid keeps for himself, deep within his fortress."

"At your command, my prince," Igneous said, "my legions will ride out and take it from the villain."

Before Lumen could reply, the Oracle said, "You are brave, my Spider Riders, but to ride directly into the lair of Mantid would be disaster. He expects it."

"Do you have a plan for assaulting Mantid's fortress, great Oracle?" Lumen asked.

"The future remains unclear for now," she replied. "When the next shard is regained, my second sight will sharpen."

"We'll get the next shard, then," Hunter said.

Corona nodded. "And the next after that as well."

The Oracle smiled. "My brave children," she said. "I wish you well. Go now. I shall replenish my strength and then relay my insights to Prince Lumen."

The prince and the other Turandot bowed as the Oracle's light faded. An angry glare from Igneous reminded Hunter to bow as well.

"I'm still not used to these Turandot ceremonies!" Hunter thought, scolding himself.

"Better *get* used to them," said Shadow's voice in his mind. "I know you're an Earthen, but you're here now—and no one *ever* leaves the Inner World."

Hunter nodded to his unseen friend. In the deepest part of his mind, though, a part so deep that even Shadow couldn't see, Hunter thought, "One day, I *will* return home!"

Several sleeps later, Hunter lay on his bed, staring at the ceiling of his sparsely furnished chamber in the fortress. The room was halfway up a cliff face and accessible only via a long, narrow stairway. It had taken Hunter a while to get used to climbing up here, but now it almost felt like home.

He wished he had some posters to spruce the place up a bit, but the Turandot didn't have posters. Corona's room did have some nice wall paintings. Someone in her family had done them—someone who'd grown too old to be a Spider Rider anymore.

Hunter gazed from the ceiling to the room's only interesting feature—the cubbyholes that took up one entire wall: his trophy case. Every Spider Rider room had one; most were filled with hard-won Insector life force medallions. The Spider Riders prized the medallions above all other things, except for their manacles and armor. Each trophy represented a rider victory and an Insector defeat.

Hunter had gained only one medallion during his time in Arachnia. The one he had, though, was very significant. It belonged to Centok, the Centipedian commander who had led the recent assault against Arachnia. Centok's lightning thrower had nearly brought the city walls tumbling down.

Hunter had defeated Centok, though he hadn't actually been able to claim the medallion himself. Igneous or one of the others had removed it for him. At the time, Hunter had been unconscious, gravely wounded in the final battle.

Hunter gazed at the medallion and sighed.

Sure, he'd been instrumental in defeating Centok and the Centipedian army, but displaying the medallion still didn't feel quite right. Because he hadn't claimed it himself, Hunter felt as though he hadn't really earned it.

"That's nonsense," said Shadow's voice inside his head. "You won that medallion, even if you didn't pull it off Centok's carapace yourself. Everyone thought you were amazingly clever and brave, even me. Even Ebony—and you know how hard the prince's spider is to please."

Hunter frowned, wishing that the compound where the battle spiders relaxed while in the city were just a bit farther away from his sleeping quarters.

"I heard that, too," Shadow said. "You really have to concentrate if you want to keep me out of your thoughts."

"I don't want to concentrate," Hunter said aloud. "I want to relax!" He wished the spider were actually in the room, so that he could throw a pillow at him.

"That's a fine thing to think!" huffed Shadow. "Maybe I should throw some webs your direction next time I see you— just on principle. Someone's at the door, by the way."

Hunter sighed again. The Spider Riders often used their spiders to send arrival messages as they stood outside one another's chambers. He wished the riders would just take up the custom of knocking.

"Come in!" he called, not bothering to ask Shadow who was waiting outside.

Corona lifted the edge of Hunter's privacy curtain and stepped into the room. The never-setting sun of the Inner World blazed into the darkened chamber.

The bright orange light made Hunter squint, but he smiled anyway. Corona smiled back at him and sat down on a wooden chair with a cushion made of spider silk near the trophy wall.

"What's up?" Hunter asked.

Corona glanced at the ceiling and then back down, as she quickly remembered that "What's up?" was just one of Hunter's Earthen expressions. She took a deep breath and gazed very seriously at him.

"I've been reassigned," she said.

Hunter's jaw dropped.

"The prince has put me in command of Petra's old squad."

"The Lost Legion?" Hunter asked.

"Yes," Corona replied, "though I hope we won't be living up to that nickname."

Petra's group of riders had been trapped and imprisoned in the caves of the Snowmites. Previously, the small unit had been known as Petra's legion. Since the Snowmite incident, they'd been known as the Lost Legion.

"I hope so, too," Hunter said. "I mean…I hope not. I mean…" He puffed out a long breath and shrugged. "You know what I mean."

Corona nodded and smiled slightly. "I've been training with the squad since we got back. Prince Lumen asked me to keep it secret. I'm sorry. I wanted to tell you earlier."

"That's okay," Hunter said. "I understand."

He looked earnestly at Corona. "I…I'll miss you," he said. "I kind of count on you protecting my back."

"I count on you as well," she replied. "We'll get used to working with other people, though. I'm sure the Oracle knows best."

"I'm sure she does, too," Hunter said. "But does Prince Lumen?"

Corona stood and her demeanor stiffened. "It is not our place to question the prince," she said.

"Yeah, that's what I thought, too, until Igneous blamed me for His Worship's mistakes," Hunter replied. "I should have gone down into that pit after the shard—not the prince. But Lumen ordered me to let him retrieve it."

"You might not have survived the security traps," Corona pointed out. "The prince has special perceptions, a knack for hidden passageways. Perhaps the Oracle did the choosing."

"Yeah," Hunter said, "except Igneous still blames me for messing up. What's up with that guy? I never seem to be able to please him."

"Igneous has exacting standards," Corona said. "Though Lumen commands the riders, it is up to Igneous to make sure the prince's plans are successful."

Hunter stood and paced. "I know, I know. Sometimes it seems like I'm treated differently from the others, though."

"You are an Earthen," Corona reminded him. "That makes you different."

"Not *that* different. I don't see Igneous chewing out you or Magma all the time—and Magma's still technically a mercenary."

Corona looked sympathetic. "A *very experienced* mercenary," she reminded him. "Hunter, don't worry. You're becoming a fine Spider Rider. Igneous will come to trust you. You just need to give him time."

Hunter nodded and sighed. "Yeah," he said. "I guess." Deep in his mind, he thought, "Maybe he'll trust me by the time I'm ready to go home."

Corona patted him on the shoulder. "You'll do it, Hunter," she said reassuringly. "I know you will."

Hunter was stunned for a moment. Had she read his innermost thought? But no. Humans could only read one another's thoughts through their spiders, and only when the spiders wanted them to. Corona must have been referring to winning Igneous's confidence.

"Igneous is at the door," Shadow said in Hunter's mind.

Venus told Corona as well. Hunter and Corona turned as the Spider Rider leader entered.

"Corona," Igneous said, not appearing at all surprised to see her there, "shouldn't you be readying your squad for their mission?"

"I was just about to," she replied. "I came to say good-bye to Hunter, first."

"Good-bye?" Hunter said, crestfallen.

"It may be a while before we see each other again," Corona explained.

"How long?" he asked.

"That depends on how my mission turns out," she said, "and how yours turns out as well."

"Which is why I'm here," Igneous said. "Get your gear, Earthen. We're off to find the next shard."

6
Misfits

Hunter rode across the desolate plains between the jungle and the sandblasted land of the Centipedians. Shadow covered the terrain with astonishing quickness, running nearly as fast as a surface-world automobile.

Usually, riding on spiderback at top speed thrilled Hunter to his core. Usually, though, Corona and Venus would have been riding beside him. Hunter's companions, Magma and Igneous, were great warriors, and their spiders—Brutus and Flame—were among the strongest in Arachnia, but they were scant substitute for the friendly Turandot girl.

Igneous and Magma weren't really Hunter's friends, not like Corona. Igneous remained cold and distant, barely speaking to Hunter at all, unless it was to criticize something. Magma tolerated the Earthen boy with good humor, but he didn't really seem to take Hunter seriously.

"Magma likes you," Shadow commented. "That's just his way. He's all bluster and brute force. Brutus is the same. You just have to get to know them."

"Well, pardon me if I don't have telepathy to tell me what people are really like," Hunter replied.

"You wouldn't need telepathy if you weren't being moody all the time," Shadow shot back.

"Look who's talking! And I'm *not* moody all the time—just right now."

"It's always 'now' somewhere," Shadow thought. "Magma likes you fine. Trust me."

"Well, Igneous doesn't like me," Hunter said.

"Corona is right," Shadow replied. "You have to earn his respect."

"I thought I did that when I won the battle with the Centipedians!"

"One battle does not a war make," Shadow observed.

Hunter groaned silently. "Spare me the spider philosophy!"

"Quiet, you two!" Igneous called from atop a nearby ridge. He'd gone ahead to scout. "Flame says he can hear the buzz of you arguing all the way over here!"

"I hope Flame can't hear what we're arguing about!" Hunter told Shadow.

"Don't worry," the spider replied. "I was masking the conversation a bit, even if you weren't."

Magma rode up beside Hunter and Shadow. "Igneous is right," he said. An almost-sympathetic smile creased his angular face. "Anyone with telepathic abilities would know you two were coming a half day off."

"I thought only Spider Riders and their spiders had telepathy," Hunter said.

"That's a common misconception among the young," Magma replied. "Some powerful Insectors can read minds, too. Or, if not read minds, then hear the buzz of rider and spider talking."

"There are rogue spiders and rogue Spider Riders, too," Brutus added, his deep voice suddenly ringing clearly in Hunter's head.

"There are?" Hunter asked.

"Not many, but some," Magma confirmed. "So it's best to watch yourself."

"Stray thoughts slay Turandot," Hunter said thoughtfully.

Magma folded his arms over his massive chest and nodded. "That's a wise adage. Who taught it to you?"

"Corona," Hunter replied. "I wish she were here."

Magma laughed. "If wishes were webs, we'd all live in Valeria!" Brutus and Shadow joined in the laughter.

Hunter nodded and laughed along, as though he understood the reference. But in the deepest recesses of his mind, where even Shadow couldn't hear him, he thought, "Will I ever fit in here?"

Princess Sparkle sighed. "Some days, I don't think Lumen and the rest will ever let me become a Spider Rider!" Cautiously, she peered out of the secret passageway leading from her bedroom toward the castle's outer precincts.

"Princess..." Hotarla whined telepathically, "we *really* shouldn't be doing this!"

"Pipe down!" Sparkle replied. "You're thinking so loud, it's a wonder every spider on the plateau can't hear you! Do you *want* us to get caught?"

"M-maybe," Hotarla replied. The spider's concerned tones echoed inside Sparkle's head.

"That's a fine thing to say!" Sparkle thought back.

"But, mistress," Hotarla said, "you are *not* officially a Spider Rider, and you are *not* old enough to safely manage the Forge by yourself, and—"

"And it is *not* your place to tell me what to do!" the princess thought back sharply. "I am second in line to the throne of Arachnia. I'm tired of them treating me like I'm not even there. I'm tired of being left behind. I need to be able to help my brother and the kingdom."

"Even if he does not want your help?" Hotarla asked gently.

Sparkle frowned at her arachnid companion. The spider was larger than Sparkle, but not nearly so large as a full-grown battle spider.

Hotarla's armored face didn't change, but Sparkle felt her frowning back. It was times like these that the princess wished that she and her spider weren't so closely linked.

"That's a fine thing to think!" Hotarla said. "I suppose you'd be happier without a spider of your own!"

Sparkle threw her arms around the big arachnid. "Of course not, Hotarla!" she thought. "You're brave and strong and…"

Hotarla sulked. "Not so strong and brave as you'd like, it seems—even with all our training!"

Sparkle straightened up. "Well," she thought, "prove to me how brave you are, then. I *know* we can handle the Forge on our own. We've seen it used hundreds of times. I *know* we can help my brother—even if he doesn't know it yet."

"And I suppose we can help Hunter Steele, too," Hotarla thought.

Sparkle reddened slightly. "I guess… If he needs helping."

Hotarla's sigh echoed through Sparkle's mind. "Very well," the spider said. "I suppose you'll do it even if I don't help. Let's go, then."

"Thanks, Hotarla!" Sparkle said, giving her eight-legged friend a quick hug.

The princess and the spider strode quickly through the corridors of the great palace in Arachnia. Sparkle held her chin up and kept her eyes focused squarely ahead. She hoped that if she looked regal enough, no one would question where the two of them were going or what they intended to do— even though it was sleep time and nearly everyone in the castle was abed. Hotarla scurried along behind the princess, looking warily from side to side. The spider's continuous misgivings echoed in Sparkle's brain.

"Don't worry," Sparkle thought resolutely. "I *know* we can do this."

When they reached the correct courtyard, they hurried across it to the great marble building that housed the Forge of the Spider Riders. The huge doors of the edifice were sealed for the city's sleep period, but Sparkle—as a member of the royal family—knew the secret of opening them. She quickly pressed the eight eyes of the spider-shaped lock in the correct sequence. The doors opened, and she and Hotarla slipped inside.

"Now, you know what you have to do?" Sparkle asked Hotarla, feeling nervous despite herself.

"We've gone over it a hundred times," Hotarla thought back. "Let's hurry and load the cauldron. I want to get this over with before anyone finds us."

Hotarla and Sparkle hurried to the room where captured Insector armor, raw material for the Forge, was stored. It seemed to take ages to drag the heavy pieces they needed for their plan to the cauldron to be melted. By the time they'd carried enough, both spider and girl were nearly exhausted.

"It's a good thing the Forge's fires are always lit," Sparkle said. "I don't think the keepers would approve of what we're doing." She grinned mischievously.

"Activate your armor, and let's get it over with before we're discovered," Hotarla thought.

Princess Sparkle gripped the metal, spider-shaped manacle on her arm and whispered, "Arachna might!"

Instantly, the bracelet transformed into gleaming armor.

Sparkle stepped forward between the two halves of a giant metal cocoon—the Forge. The cocoon closed around Sparkle, and the spider-shaped cauldron above tipped forward, spilling molten armor into the Forge.

As the heat blazed around her, Sparkle concentrated hard on the new power she wanted to add to her manacle. Outside the Forge, Hotarla focused all her will on the same task.

The Forge glowed white with power. Then the glow dimmed, and the two halves of the Forge slid silently open.

Sparkle stepped out, smiling and looking very tired. "I think we did it!" she enthused.

"Try it out," Hotarla said. She looked around nervously. "I think I hear someone coming!"

Princess Sparkle climbed onto her spider's back and pressed the new, gemlike stud on her manacle. She concentrated hard on making the power activate. As she did, the doors to the Forge room swung open, and the man and woman who tended the Forge entered.

The couple looked as though they'd just woken up; they also looked very concerned.

"What's going on here?" the man asked. He scanned the room with his dark, serious eyes.

"I thought I heard the Forge activate," the woman replied.

The man sniffed the air. "It's hot enough," he said.

The woman peered around the darkened chamber. "But no one's here," she said.

Both of them looked puzzled as, unnoticed, Sparkle and Hotarla hurried from the room.

"They couldn't see us at all!" Hotarla thought excitedly.

"We did it!" Sparkle mind-talked back. "We got the power we wanted. We can become invisible!"

"How far off are they?" Stags rumbled.

"They're close. Very close," Dungobeet replied. A single messenger bug circled his head before whizzing off into the distance once more. "You see?" the beetleoid continued, "I told you that they would come for the next shard. If you can slay them…"

"Yes," Stags replied, stroking one massive claw against his bony chin, "that would redeem me in Mantid's eyes."

"Though the Centipedians losing their shard was hardly your fault," Dungo added.

"Mantid would not forgive me, even if it wasn't my fault," Stags said. "Of course, were our places reversed, I would not forgive him, either."

Dungobeet nodded. "And do you think that might be possible?" he asked. "I mean, your places being reversed."

Stags smiled a wicked smile. "Such things have been known to happen," he said, "given time."

Dungobeet smiled back. "And given success," he added.

"Yes," Stags hissed thoughtfully. "The deaths of these Riders will be the first stepping-stone on my road to ultimate power."

"That being the case, your lordship," Dungo said, "I hope you will remember who made this day possible."

Stags scowled at the smaller Insector. "What do you mean, bug?" he asked. "It is my boldness that has made this ambush possible." He clacked his claws and gnashed his huge mandibles menacingly.

Fearing Stags might take his head off, Dungobeet bowed. "Of course, your lordship," he said. "Now, if you'll excuse me, sire, Lord Mantid has ordered me back to his fortress."

Stags nodded imperiously. "Slink away before the battle if you must, coward," he said. "I alone will prepare my forces." A wicked smile crossed the huge Insector's armored face. "Soon the accursed Spider Riders will die!"

7
Ambushed!

"What do you think Corona's up to right now?" Hunter asked Shadow. He and his spider were riding down a long valley between rocky hills. They were descending from the desolate plains toward the great ocean, but they still had a long way to go. Hunter's armor felt heavy, and he was bored.

Magma and Igneous rode beside Hunter, standing on the backs of their spiders as they went. The two looked like armored surfers, trying to outride each other on a speeding wave. They grinned at each other and nodded appreciatively as one or the other of them crossed a particularly difficult piece of terrain without so much as a wobble.

Hunter had gotten pretty good at riding standing up—even when he didn't need to do so to fight—but he didn't have time for Spider Rider games now. The two older riders remained oblivious to the fact that Hunter's thoughts—at the moment—had nothing to do with either their fancy riding or their objective.

"I have no idea what Corona's up to now," Shadow thought back. "She's on a secret mission. That's the whole point of it—it's *secret*."

"But you could ask Venus what they were doing if you wanted to," Hunter said. "What's the range on spider mind talk, anyway?"

"It varies by skill and age," Shadow said. "I could hear my master, Darkness, from many leagues away."

Hunter heard the sadness in his friend's voice and remembered the death of the great spider who had been Shadow's mentor.

"But what about Venus?" Hunter thought, trying to keep the tone of their mind-talk conversation light. "How far away do you think you could talk to her?"

"We're not supposed to contact her," Shadow insisted.

"So, then, you couldn't do it now," Hunter said.

"I could if I wanted," Shadow replied peevishly. "But she's on a *secret* mission!"

"Well, if you can't do it," Hunter replied, shrugging, "just say so."

"I'm *not* saying—" Shadow began. "Look out!"

"You're not saying 'look out'?" Hunter asked.

Shadow flattened himself to the ground as a volley of arrows sailed over their heads. Hunter nearly fell off the spider's back. He cursed himself for being so worried about Corona that he'd nearly been killed himself.

"Centipedians!" Magma shouted. "It's an ambush!"

Igneous glared at Hunter. "I told you two to keep your mind talk quiet!" he said.

Magma and Brutus leaped aside just as the ground collapsed under their feet, revealing a deep, concealed pit running across the rocky valley floor. Flame dug the bony spurs of his armor into the ground. Dust and rubble kicked into the air. He and Igneous halted just inches from the pit's edge. Magma and Brutus somersaulted in the air and landed several yards behind the Spider Rider leader.

"I can't stop!" Shadow thought desperately.

"Jump the way Brutus did!" Hunter thought.

"I haven't mastered that maneuver!" Shadow replied. He gathered his legs to leap forward across the expanse.

But Hunter spotted something that Shadow hadn't seen. "No!" he cried. "That's what they want! Use your web!"

Hunter's message was so urgent that Shadow didn't question it. In an instant, he anchored a web line to a nearby boulder. The line snapped taut, and Shadow and Hunter jerked to a stop at the edge of the pit. The boulder lurched under the big spider's weight but held tight.

Hunter and Shadow looked down. Sharp spikes filled the bottom of the pit. If they'd fallen in, even their armor might not have been enough to protect them.

Shadow crept back from the edge of the pit. "Why couldn't I just jump it?" he asked Hunter.

"Look!" Hunter replied. He concentrated and sent a low-power sonic charge out to the other side of the chasm.

The charge blasted through the air and shook the ground on the other side of the pit. As it did, the earth there gave way as well, revealing a second pit full of spikes.

"They wanted us to jump the first pit…" Hunter began.

"So we'd fall into the second," Shadow said. "I understand."

"Good thing I have sharp eyes," Hunter added.

"That's not the only sharp thing you'll have if you're not careful," Shadow replied. "Duck!"

Hunter did as a second volley of Centipedian spears and arrows flashed over his head. As they did, armored Centipedians rushed out from concealed holes in the valley walls.

Igneous and Magma, who hadn't come as close to crashing into the pit as Hunter had, drew their stun swords and rushed the Insectors' front lines. Brutus and Flame fought magnificently, plowing through the ranks of the advancing 'pedes and felling even more with their sleep darts.

Magma's war cry echoed across the valley. "Hizz-ahhh!"

Hunter and Shadow leaped after them, cutting off a group of Insectors trying to outflank the other Spider Riders.

"Sonic charge!" Hunter shouted, leveling a blast into the Centipedians rushing at him. The deafening peal of his weapon shook the air, and the 'pedes scattered like tenpins.

"Save your manacle power!" Igneous thundered in his mind. "We'll need it for the mission."

Hunter frowned. "But there won't be any mission if we don't get rid of these 'pedes!" he thought back, unsure if Igneous would hear him.

"Do what Igneous says," Shadow cautioned. "Flame says to trust him."

"Well, Flame *would* say that," Hunter shot back. "They work together, after all!" He brought up his sword just in time to parry the fangs of a charging 'pede, aimed at his neck.

He turned the parry into a slash and struck the 'pede between the eyes. The monster reeled back, stunned.

"Riders and spiders don't always agree," Shadow noted, "as you well know." He quickly webbed the fallen 'pede.

"Less talk, more fighting!" Hunter thought back. He activated the shield on his manacle just in time to fend off a half dozen arrows hurtling in their direction.

Shadow leaped into the line of 'pede archers as they reloaded. The spider's eight legs flashed out, toppling a dozen archers while Hunter knocked out another half dozen with his sword. Shadow stung two more with sleep darts.

"Good work, riders!" Igneous called. He and Magma had thrashed nearly enough 'pedes to break the Insectors' line. "Keep fighting!"

"As if we were going to suddenly give up," Hunter muttered.

"Careful," Shadow warned. "I think Flame heard that."

"So-rry!" Hunter replied. "Hey, watch our backs!"

Shadow turned just as another set of 'pedes rushed out from under their camouflaged rocks. The spider lunged into them, knocking most of them down. Hunter stunned the rest.

"They're not so tough!" Shadow thought. "I'm surprised they dared to take us on without some kind of tough-guy war leader."

Movement on the rocky ridge nearby caught Hunter's attention. "Um, maybe they *did* bring a leader with them," he said.

As he spoke, Stags appeared atop the ridge. Behind him, pushed by many centipede warriors, came a lightning thrower.

Stags smiled and aimed the weapon toward the embattled Spider Riders. The big Insector showed no concern for his own forces, who were desperately trying to surround the human riders.

"He wouldn't shoot through his own troops just to kill *us*!" Hunter thought.

"Oh yes, he would!" Shadow replied. "I'll warn the others!" He thought something so quickly that Hunter caught only a faint buzz.

The lightning thrower began to glow as energy built up within it.

"Form up!" Igneous commanded, his thought so loud that Hunter winced.

"Shouldn't we scatter to give them fewer targets?" Hunter asked. But Shadow was already hurrying to join the other spiders in a tight formation.

Hunter wedged his feet tightly into the stirruplike spiracles in Shadow's armor to avoid being swept off as the spider charged forward.

Two Centipedians sprang up between Hunter and Shadow, and the rest of the Spider Riders. Hunter stood, assuming a classic Spider Rider attack posture. His stun sword flashed quickly left and right, knocking the Centipedians aside as he and Shadow fell in beside Brutus and Flame.

"Shields up!" Igneous said.

Instantly, all three Spider Riders activated the manacle-powered shields on their wrists.

Stags's minions heaved, using their many arms and legs to quickly swing the lightning thrower around. They aimed the cannon directly at the three Spider Riders. The Insectors followed Stags's orders, not caring that many of their own comrades stood in the way.

"Angle your shield toward the lightning thrower," Shadow thought to Hunter. "Igneous will use some of his manacle power to link the shields together."

"I'd already figured that out," Hunter replied, moving to complete the maneuver even before Shadow asked. "But will it be enough to keep us from getting fried?"

Before Shadow could answer, searing white energy blazed out of the lightning cannon. The Turandot spiders crouched low, presenting the smallest possible target to the lightning bolt.

The Centipedians between the weapon and the Spider Riders sensed the danger, but they couldn't get out of the way. They howled in terror as the energy seared through their ranks, blasting toward the Spider Riders. The Insector troops flew through the air as if scattered by a giant hand.

The bolt hit the combined energy shield of the Spider Riders. Forked tongues of crackling lightning danced all around them, but their shields held.

Hunter winced. He felt as if fireworks had gone off right beside his head.

"Move!" Igneous commanded.

Hunter felt dizzy, but Shadow was already executing Igneous's order.

"Where are we going?" Hunter thought, trying to regain his bearings.

"Flame says we have to try to take out the lightning thrower before it can fire again," Shadow replied.

"Okay," Hunter said. "Any idea how we're gonna do that?" He gazed out over the sea of Centipedians barring their way. The first blast of the lightning thrower had thinned the 'pedes out some but not enough to give the Spider Riders a clear path to the weapon.

The Insectors closed ranks to block the riders. Shadow, Flame, and Brutus leaped forward, bowling over a mass of the enemy. More 'pedes surged into the gaps. The Centipedians stabbed at the Spider Riders with spears and slashed at them with swords.

The battle spiders' armor turned most of the weapons aside, and the riders' flashing swords caught the rest.

Hunter glanced up apprehensively at the lightning thrower. Already it was building for another blast. Clearly, the Insectors had improved the weapon since their assault on the city of Arachnia.

"Shadow, tell Igneous—" Hunter began.

"He already knows," Shadow replied. "We're going to form up again...now!"

All three spiders jumped simultaneously, crashing into a startled band of Centipedian warriors between them and the cannon. Hunter, Igneous, and Magma linked up their shields once more, but the two wide pit traps still separated them from Stags's deadly machine.

"He can keep firing at us all day unless we can figure out some way to get across those pits," Hunter thought.

"But they're still too wide to jump," Shadow thought in reply. "And we don't have time to form web bridges."

"Well, we'd better think of something quick," Hunter said, "or all of us are dead!"

8
Burned

With a boom louder than the finale of a fireworks display, the lightning cannon blasted down into the rocky valley once more.

Having seen how little regard Stags had for the lives of his troops, this time the Centipedians nearby had sense enough to get out of the way. The lightning bolt hit far fewer of them and spent far more of its energy on the Spider Riders.

The impact from the shock nearly knocked Hunter off Shadow's back. He held on, barely, and forced himself upright once more.

"Are you all right?" Shadow asked.

"I don't want to do this too much longer," Hunter replied. He glanced at the power crystal on his manacle. It was already blinking a low-power warning. "We need a better plan," he said.

"I'm sure Igneous is open to suggestions," Shadow replied. Already he and the other spiders were moving toward the Centipedian weapon again, but the Centipedians had re-formed as well, blocking their way.

A huge scorpion charged at Igneous and Flame. Igneous batted aside one claw with his sword, but the other latched onto Flame's front leg. Centipedians swarmed in on all sides, holding the spider's other legs down.

The scorpion's deadly stinger swung toward Flame. Its poisoned barb aimed for a weak joint near the leg in the spider's armor.

"Igneous, look out!" Hunter cried.

A sudden blast of plasma ripped through the air and struck the scorpion. It shattered the beast's tail, just below the stinger.

"Good work, Magma!" Shadow thought.

The big mercenary was fighting amid a crowd of 'pedes nearby. A faint glow of energy hung in the air around Magma's power manacle. His warning light was flashing, too.

The scorpion attacking Igneous reeled back, and Flame shook free from its claws. Brutus and Magma surged forward.

Brutus grabbed the creature with his front legs and lifted the scorpion and its rider high into the air. Before the startled Insectors could react, Brutus flung them straight at the lightning thrower.

"Fire!" Stags cried, though the weapon hadn't yet built up its maximum energy.

The Centipedians obeyed, and lightning shot forth once more. It blasted the scorpion and its rider before they could strike the weapon. The victims' charred bodies smashed against the hillside and tumbled to the ground.

Magma smiled. "That bought us some time," he said, riding up close to Hunter.

"Bought us some time to do what?" Hunter replied.

"Spray a wall of webs between us and the cannon," Igneous ordered. "It will slow the 'pedes down and make us more difficult to hit with the lightning."

Hunter nodded, remembering how Shadow's web had short-circuited the previous Insector lightning thrower. They weren't close enough to try that trick again, but maybe a wall of webs could offer them some protection.

Reflexively, he glanced at his manacle's blinking power crystal.

"Don't worry," Shadow reminded him. "Spinning webs doesn't require manacle power."

"I know," Hunter replied. "I'm just not sure how many more lightning blasts we can fend off."

The Turandot spiders bounded through the ranks of Centipedians, spraying webs everywhere. Very quickly, the Insector army bogged down in the sticky strands.

Hunter rode up beside Igneous. "That'll give us some more time," he said, "but now the 'pedes are tangled up between us and the lightning thrower. How will we destroy the weapon if we can't reach it?"

"I'm open to suggestions," Igneous replied. "Until then, keep spinning."

Hunter and the rest kept spinning as the lightning thrower built up another charge. They piled the tangled Centipedians on top of one another, building a living wall between themselves and the deadly cannon.

The weapon fired again. The thunder of its discharge shook the air and made Hunter's head throb.

The wall of Centipedians toppled with a hideous crunching sound. The wounded Insectors wailed and writhed on the ground. Standing atop the rise, Stags merely smiled.

"What now?" Magma asked Igneous. All of their power crystals were flashing weakly. None had much manacle energy remaining.

"I'll show you," Igneous said. He and Flame surged forward, toward the rift in the wall of bodies. Suddenly, the Spider Rider leader powered down his armor.

"Stags!" he called up to the beetleoid commander. "We surrender!"

"What!" Hunter, Magma, and their spiders all cried simultaneously.

Igneous looked sternly at them. "We're outnumbered, which would be bad enough," he said, "but we can't fight Stags's lightning thrower. Surrender is our only choice. Put away your swords."

Stags laughed. "I always knew you Spider Riders were cowards at heart," he said.

"What's going on here?" Hunter asked Shadow.

"I don't know," Shadow replied. Hunter could feel the spider's confusion through their mind link.

"I said, put away your swords!" Igneous repeated. "This is a fight we can't win."

Reluctantly, Hunter and Magma did as their leader commanded, though neither of them deactivated his armor. Magma's eyes burned with fury.

Igneous turned back to Stags. "We surrender," he repeated. "We throw ourselves on your mercy, great Stags."

The hulking beetleoid's armored face broke into a wicked smile.

"I thought you soft-fleshed Turandot would know by now," the Insector leader said, "I don't have any mercy." He gestured for his Centipedian troops, who had been decimated by the Spider Riders' attack, to move forward and surround the riders and their mounts.

Slowly, the 'pedes brandished their weapons and moved in.

"Well?" Stags bellowed. "What are you waiting for? They're surrounded. Finish them!"

"They're waiting for their leader to smarten up," Igneous said, a smile breaking across his grim face.

Stags looked confused. "What?" he boomed.

Hunter and Shadow felt just as confused as the Insector commander, but Magma merely laughed.

"Igneous is right, beetle brain," he said. "Those 'pedes have more sense than their leader. They know it's not we who are surrounded…it's you!"

As he spoke, four more Spider Riders appeared atop the ridge on either side of the Insector general.

"Corona!" Hunter cried.

Before Stags and his lieutenants could react, Corona and the Lost Legion sprang on them. The four new riders knocked aside the guards atop the ridge and headed for the lightning thrower. The guards tumbled down the slope, screaming, and fell into the pit they had intended as a trap for Igneous's squad.

Hunter drew his sword. "She was following us all along," Shadow told him.

"Igneous or the prince must have gotten wind of this trap, somehow," Hunter concluded.

Igneous, riding nearby in full armor once more, heard him. "Some of us did know how to do our jobs before you came along, Earthen," he said.

Hunter turned slightly red, vowing to use only mind talk for his musings from now on. He thrashed a nearby

Centipedian with his sword as Shadow used sleep darts on two more.

"I wish Corona had told us," Hunter thought to his spider.

"I don't think anyone but Igneous knew," Shadow replied. "Remember, the Oracle sensed that an evil telepath is working against us."

Shadow leaped forward, landing just a few yards from a mounted Centipedian who was trying to rally the enemy forces. Hunter sheathed his sword and used his manacle to quickly summon up his jousting lance.

The Centipedian and its scorpion mount turned toward Hunter and Shadow—a moment too late.

Hunter's lance slammed into the 'pede's chest. The Insector flew off the scorpion's back, landed hard against a nearby boulder, and slumped to the ground.

The scorpion wobbled from the impact of the blow. Shadow ducked under it and heaved. The stunned giant insect toppled backward into one of the big Centipedian trenches intended to trap the riders.

"Nice work," Hunter thought, flourishing his battle lance. "Looks like those trenches are working for us instead of for our enemy."

"Don't pat yourself on the back too hard," Shadow thought back. "Corona needs our help."

A rumble like distant thunder filled the valley. Atop the ridge on the far side of the pits, Corona was battling Stags and a dozen Centipedians. All of them were standing atop the lightning thrower, fighting for control of the deadly machine.

As Hunter and Shadow watched in horror, the lightning thrower slid down the slope toward the pit. Several of the Centipedians fell off as the machine skidded down. Corona and Venus barely managed to keep their footing as rocks and dirt cascaded all around them.

Corona looked for a way out, but the landslide upslope made escape that way impossible. Stags, his armored face a mask of hatred and rage, scrambled over the skidding weapon toward Corona.

"Venus should jump this way," Hunter said. He clouted a row of Centipedians to their right with his lance.

"Venus can't jump that far," Shadow replied. "They dug the ditches too wide for spiders to jump." He knocked four 'pedes down with his legs and broke the spear of another with his mandibles.

"She can if we help her," Hunter replied. "Get us as close to the edge of the pit as you can."

Shadow quickly ran in the direction Hunter indicated. As they reached the edge of the yawning trap, Hunter powered up his manacle and pointed it toward the far side.

"Sonic charge!" he cried.

Screaming bursts of sonic energy streaked from his manacle to the far side of the pit. Rocks shattered and tumbled down the slope, forming a lip at the pit's edge. As the front of the lightning thrower hit the lip, the weapon's back end pitched forward into the air.

The lightning thrower tumbled up straight, like a pole-vaulter's pole. Just as the weapon passed vertical, Venus leaped. The extra height and momentum she gained from the makeshift vault carried her over the edge of the Centipedian trap. Flame, who had been alerted to the plan by Shadow, spun a soft web net for Corona and her spider to land in.

"Yes!" Hunter said, pumping his fist in the air.

But his plan had worked too well. The lightning thrower also vaulted the trap. It crashed into the side of the pit nearest to Hunter and Shadow. A huge cloud of dust shot into the air, and the ground shook beneath them. Suddenly, the ledge they were standing on gave way.

Before they could even call for help, Shadow and Hunter toppled into the pit.

9
Hunter vs. Stags

Stones and dirt rained down around the startled Hunter and Shadow as the two of them slid into the darkness.

"Use your webs to slow us down!" Hunter cried in mind talk.

"What do you think I'm doing?" Shadow replied. "The dirt's too loose to latch onto!"

The two of them tumbled end over end into the trench. Hunter lost his footing, fell off Shadow's back, and landed on something hard. The air rushed out of his lungs with a hearty "Oof!"

"I'll second that," Shadow thought.

Hunter could feel his spider's pain. "Shadow, are you all right?" he asked.

"Just bruised," Shadow replied, getting to his feet. "I'm wondering why the spikes at the bottom of the pit didn't kill us."

Hunter got up as well. "Yeah. Me, too." The dust filling the air made it almost impossible to see. Hunter knelt back down and ran his fingers over the hard object below them.

"I think we landed on part of the lightning thrower," he said. "It probably saved our lives."

"That's an ironic twist," Shadow thought, using an expression he'd learned from Hunter.

Hunter tried to summon a light from his manacle, but the bracelet's power was completely depleted. He waved the dust away from his face and remounted Shadow. The sounds of the battle continuing above echoed down the pit to them.

"We have to get out of here," Hunter said.

"I'll be happy to," Shadow replied, "as soon as you tell me which way to go without being skewered."

"Up might be safe, if we can find the wall," Hunter suggested.

"No way is safe!" a deep voice boomed. "You and your accursed spider will die here—by my hand."

Shadow and Hunter turned and saw Stags emerging from the dust cloud. The Insector general's armor looked scuffed but little the worse for wear. A battle scorpion, probably the one they'd knocked into the pit earlier, scrambled to Stags's side. Stags mounted up and unslung a huge battle-ax from his back.

"What does it take to kill this guy?" Shadow thought.

"It's time to find out," Hunter thought back. Instinctively, he tried to power up his lance; it didn't work.

"Out of manacle energy, remember?" Shadow said.

Hunter nodded and said, "Then I guess we'll just have to do this the old-fashioned way."

At Hunter's mental command, the huge battle spider shot forward. Hunter leveled his lance at Stags's chest, just as Igneous had taught him.

Hunter had jousted with Insectors before, and he'd jousted many times in the practice ring. He'd never faced an opponent like Stags, though.

The giant beetleoid maneuvered his battle scorpion with surprising quickness. As Hunter and Shadow bore in, the scorpion sidestepped and grabbed Hunter's lance in its left claw.

The scorpion pulled, and Hunter barely kept his seat. As Hunter lurched forward, Stags swung his ax at Hunter's head. Shadow dodged away, yanking Hunter out of the ax's reach, but Hunter lost hold of his lance in the process.

"Great!" Hunter blurted, meaning just the opposite.

Stags laughed and swung again, but Shadow kept them out of the way.

"That scorpion will snap my lance in two if we don't get it back," Hunter thought.

"And he'll snap your neck if we're not careful," Shadow replied. Keeping his footing on the rubble-strewn bottom of the pit was proving tricky for the spider.

The dust had cleared a bit, revealing the dangerous nature of the surrounding terrain. Many sharp spikes, hard enough to penetrate even battle armor, jutted up from the wreckage strewn across the floor of the pit. Every time Shadow moved, loose rocks threatened to topple him onto the spikes. Unfortunately, Stags and his scorpion mount had landed on a more solid portion of the landslide.

"Draw your sword as I move in," Shadow said. "Look for the weak spot in the hinge of the scorpion's left pincer. Hit it, and he'll drop your lance."

Hunter silently agreed.

Stags and his mount rushed forward. The Insector leader swung his ax in a wide arc, and the scorpion flailed its right pincer while applying crushing pressure to Hunter's lance with the other.

Shadow bolted forward, appearing to meet the charge head-on. At the last instant, he darted to the left, toward the scorpion's occupied claw.

Hunter drew his sword and stabbed with one fluid movement. The point pierced the softer carapace between the scorpion's upper and lower pincers. The claw opened reflexively, and Hunter's lance toppled out. He scooped it up before it hit the ground and then sheathed his sword.

He mentally congratulated Shadow. "Good plan!"

"Naturally!"

Stags growled a curse at them. "Fight like Insectors, you cowards!" He rushed at Hunter and Shadow again.

"You mean clumsily?" Hunter asked as Shadow dodged out of the way.

Stags's reply was an incoherent snarl. He whirled and charged to attack again.

Shadow would have moved out of the way, but he'd accidentally backed up too far. The pit's deadly spikes blocked his way.

"Jump over him!" Hunter thought.

"The scorpion will sting us as we do," Shadow replied. In his friend's mind, Hunter saw the spider's loathing of scorpions. "You'll have to fight it out with Stags until we can scuttle past," Shadow concluded.

Hunter gritted his teeth and turned his lance to face the charge.

The scorpion snapped at Hunter's weapon as the two enemies met. Hunter deftly moved the lance out of the way, but he couldn't bring the long spear to bear on Stags.

Stags sliced at one of Shadow's legs, but the weapon glanced off the battle spider's armor.

Shadow hissed and rammed the scorpion. He grabbed one of the scorpion's legs in his mandibles and snapped it. The

69

scorpion shrieked and reared back. Stags lurched but didn't lose his seat.

Hunter stabbed at the scorpion with his lance, but the point slid past the creature's armor. Stags smashed at the lance with his ax. The long spear didn't break, but the shock of the blow made Hunter's shoulder throb.

"Duck!" Shadow thought.

Hunter did and the scorpion's stinger barely missed his head. He remembered the time a scorpion sting had nearly killed Corona and swallowed hard. Only quick action by the other Spider Riders had kept her from dying that day. Here in the pit, there would be no one to save him with a manacle's healing touch.

"Back away!" he thought. "We need some distance so I can use my lance properly."

"Easier said than done," Shadow replied.

Enraged by the loss of its limb, the scorpion moved more quickly than ever. It snapped with its claws and lashed with its tail. Shadow fended off the first two blows and barely got them out of the way of the third. When the battle spider stepped aside, he put himself and Hunter right in the path of Stags's ax.

Hunter swung his lance around barely in time. He caught the blow just above the spear's hand guard. Sparks flew where the two weapons met and jammed together.

Sweat dripped from Hunter's brow and splattered onto the chest plate of his armor.

"What's the matter, larva?" Stags growled at him. "Too small to play with the adults?"

Hunter shoved forward with all his might, but Stags barely moved. The big Insector jerked his weapon loose and cut at Hunter's neck.

Hunter might have been hit, but Shadow dodged aside just in time. "This isn't working!" Hunter thought.

"You're telling me?" Shadow replied. During the clash, he'd managed to work his way out of the corner they'd been trapped in, but several long scratches from the scorpion's claws traced across Shadow's sleek black armor.

"We'll never outlast this brute," Hunter thought. "So we'll have to outthink him."

"We are in deep trouble, then!" Shadow quipped.

As they tried to regain their breaths, Stags and the scorpion came in again.

"I have an idea!" Hunter thought urgently. "Go with me on this."

Shadow didn't reply, but reading the plan in Hunter's mind, charged straight at their enemies. Hunter aimed his lance at Stags's chest.

The Insector leader's multifaceted eyes gleamed in anticipation of the kill. He readied his ax to parry Hunter's lance and then slay the boy.

When they were only yards apart, though, Hunter changed his target and thrust his lance between the scorpion's left-side legs—the side that already had one leg missing.

The scorpion's limbs tangled and tripped over the lance. It lurched heavily to that side.

As it did, Shadow ducked his head. He avoided the scorpion's claws and came in under the creature's body. Hunter flattened himself, barely avoiding a lethal cut from Stags.

"Heave!" Hunter cried.

Shadow planted his eight legs and heaved up with all his might.

With a terrified screech, the scorpion toppled sideways, off the rubble and onto the spikes. The deadly points pierced the creature's body. The scorpion thrashed, kicking up a great cloud of dust as its life ebbed away.

Hunter sighed with relief. At the same time, he felt sad at taking a life—even the life of an enemy.

As the dust settled, the scorpion suddenly heaved upward and Stags crawled out from beneath. His armor was scratched and pierced in places, but the Insector commander remained very much alive.

With a howl of rage, he hefted his ax and charged at Hunter and Shadow.

Instinctively, the boy and his spider charged back. Hunter lowered his lance.

The weapon crashed into the center of Stags's chest. The spear didn't pierce the Insector's tough armor, but the force of the blow carried Stags back, into a nearby boulder.

The boulder shattered, and a huge chunk landed on top of Stags's bony head. The Insector general crashed to the ground, unconscious.

Hunter wiped the sweat from his brow.

"Well done!" said a friendly voice from above.

Hunter and Shadow looked up as Corona and Venus crawled down the wall toward them. Behind Hunter's friend came the rest of the Spider Riders. All were sweating and scratched up, but apparently none had been badly hurt during the melee.

The Lost Legion and Magma were all smiling, and even Igneous looked slightly impressed. Many of them applauded as they rode down the wall to meet the victors.

"Not bad…for a beginner," said Geode, a young member of the legion. He grinned.

Magma nodded. "The kid did good, no doubt about it," he said.

"The spiders are impressed, too," Shadow added via mind talk.

"Did you polish off the rest of them?" Hunter asked the rest.

"All webbed and ready for transport back to Arachnia," Crystal, another of the legion replied.

"All except Stags," Corona concluded.

Igneous gazed at Hunter and his eyes narrowed. Flame's eyes sparked with anger.

"Well?" Igneous said. "What are you waiting for? Dispatch him!"

10
Decoys

"W-what did you say?" Hunter asked Igneous.

Igneous pointed to Stags. "Dispatch him," the Spider Rider leader commanded.

Hunter swallowed hard, put away his lance, and drew his sword. His stomach lurched queasily. Slaying an Insector in battle was one thing, but he'd never slain a helpless enemy before.

"What are you going to do with that?" Shadow asked, mentally indicating the sword.

"What do you think?" Hunter thought back angrily.

Corona put her hand on Hunter's shoulder.

"Igneous wants you to take Stags's life force medallion," she explained. "You've defeated him. It is your right."

Corona's tone remained friendly and even, but Hunter could tell that she, as well as Shadow, knew what had been in his mind. Hunter felt both relieved and embarrassed at the same time.

"I—I thought…" he began.

"Too much battle has addled his brains!" Crystal said with a laugh. "He's forgotten that Spider Riders kill only as a last resort."

The other Spider Riders chuckled sympathetically.

"Lunkhead," Shadow added.

Hunter turned red.

"Well, take your time if you want," Igneous said impatiently, "but we haven't got until next sleep. We still have a mission to accomplish."

Hunter felt puzzled. "But our manacles are out of energy. How can we possibly go to Quagmiro now? We've got to return to the city and recharge first."

"Which is exactly what the Insectors will expect us to do," Igneous said with a smile.

"Which is why that's *not* what we're doing," Magma added.

"But..." Hunter said. This whole situation was confusing. He looked at Corona, hoping she would throw him a clue.

"Everything has happened as the Oracle foresaw," she said confidently. "That's why the legion and I were here when you needed us. We have conserved the power in our manacles. My legion will transfer their energies to you before returning to Arachnia with our captives."

"You can do that?" Hunter said. He remembered the Spider Riders using their power in concert before, but this was a new trick.

"You're clever, kid," Magma said, "but you don't know everything about being a Spider Rider yet."

"Shadow," Hunter thought, "why didn't you tell me this?"

"What?" the spider replied. "You think *I* know everything? I was untamed, remember?"

Hunter remembered. Until he and Shadow were bonded, the big spider had no intention of ever taking a rider. Only the wishes of Darkness, Shadow's elder, had forced the two of them together.

"Insector spies watching the city will believe that *we* are the riders returning with captives," Igneous said. "While, in fact, it will be three of Corona's squad. That may allow us time to reach Quagmiro undetected."

"Time we'll need to successfully recover the next shard," Corona added.

"You said, three riders will return..." Hunter mused. "Corona, are you coming with us?"

She nodded and Hunter suddenly felt less confused and alone.

"Hey, you're never alone as long as I'm alive," Shadow reminded him. "But I'm glad Corona and Venus are coming, too."

"C'mon, kid, time's wastin'," Magma said. "Pull the medallion off that thug, and let's get going."

Hunter took a deep breath and nodded. The sooner they recovered the shards, the sooner Petra would be well again.

He marched to where Stags lay facedown in the rubble. On the back of the Insector's neck was a bony, disk-shaped object: the life force medallion.

Hunter had seen other riders remove medallions—he'd seen Corona dispose of a mantis that way when they first met. He'd even been given the life force medallion of Centok because he had defeated him in battle. But Hunter had never removed a medallion himself before.

Now he grasped the disk with one hand and twisted, as he'd seen Corona and the others do. The medallion didn't budge. He put both hands on it and twisted harder.

"Twist and pull," Shadow said in his mind.

Hunter did and the medallion came free from Stags's back. Hunter held it above his defeated foe and watched. Stags's body became insubstantial, turning into reddish brown mist.

The mist floated up into the medallion as though it were being sucked into a vacuum cleaner. The medallion glowed and felt slightly warm as the mist seeped into it. Finally, only a bit of reddish dust remained where once had lain the body of the mighty Stags.

Igneous nodded. "Well done," he said.

"For a beginner," Crystal added. Hunter noticed the legion rider's eyes narrow as she glanced from him to Corona.

"Is Crystal upset about something?" Hunter asked Shadow.

"I'm not getting anything from her spider, Sapphire," Shadow replied. "Venus seems to think that she's still upset about Petra's injury. Plus, I guess Crystal and Sapphire expected to take over when Petra got hurt. The members of the legion share a very close bond. To them, Corona may always be an outsider."

"Thanks," Hunter thought back. "I'm glad I didn't have to figure that out on my own."

"Telepathy has its advantages," Shadow replied.

"And sometimes disadvantages, too," Hunter thought, careful to shield that feeling from Shadow.

"Hunter, snap to it!" Igneous commanded. "The rest of us are charged up and ready to go."

"Sorry," Hunter said. "I was...enjoying the victory."

Igneous didn't seem to buy the excuse, but Hunter didn't care.

"I'm charging you up," Crystal said to Hunter. "Think you can handle it?"

Hunter nodded and Crystal took hold of his power manacle with both hands. She closed her eyes and concentrated. As she did, Hunter felt the energy flowing from her manacle into his.

At the same time, he thought he could almost feel her anger as well. Did she not want to give up that power? Did she wish that the legion were taking on this mission rather than Hunter and the rest? Maybe she thought she deserved to go along instead of Corona. Or maybe she was still miffed that their new leader was from outside the legion, as Shadow had said.

"She'll get to lead the legion back to the city at least," Shadow thought in reply. "Maybe that will cheer her up."

Crystal finished transferring the power, then turned to go.

"Wait a minute," Hunter called. He caught up to her and handed her Stags's life force medallion.

"I'd like you to take this back to my room," he said. "I know I can trust you to get it there safely."

Crystal looked puzzled. "Don't you want to put it in your trophy case yourself when you get back?"

Hunter shook his head. "We can't chance taking it with us," he said. "If the Insectors captured the medallion, they might be able to revive Stags. None of us wants that."

Crystal gazed at him for a moment. Then she nodded and smiled slightly. She tucked the life force medallion into a compartment at her waist and climbed aboard Sapphire. "Good luck, Earthen," she said.

"Thanks," Hunter replied. "You, too."

Shadow lowered his head, and Hunter climbed up the spider's mandibles to his usual position.

"Let's move out!" Igneous commanded.

The Spider Riders picked their way through the spikes and rubble and climbed back up the wall of the pit—the three legion riders on one side, heading back to Arachnia city, Igneous and the rest up the other, headed for the ocean.

As Hunter and his group galloped away, Crystal and the legion cocooned their defeated foes. The Insectors would be stored in the Cavern of Cocoons—the Spider Rider version of prison. There, a million enemy warriors, some from centuries past, slept eternally in silken pods of white.

Igneous and Magma took the lead, with Hunter and Corona riding behind. In just a few minutes, they'd ridden out of sight.

"That was a good thing you did," Corona said, "entrusting Stags's medallion to Crystal. She hasn't been very happy since I was assigned to lead their group."

"Shadow mentioned that to me," Hunter said. "I thought maybe giving the medallion to her would show how much I... the Spider Riders, I mean...trust her and value her contribution."

Corona nodded. "As I said, it was a good thing to do. Thank you."

Hunter nodded back.

They rode in silence for a while. Then Corona sighed. "To tell you the truth," she said, "I'm not any more thrilled to be leading the legion than they are to have me as commander."

"Really?" Hunter asked. "Why not?"

"I haven't been with the legion long enough to earn their trust," she said. "Plus, I'm not much good at giving orders. I'm fine at following a strong leader like Igneous, but being one? I just don't know if I'm cut out for it." She shook her head.

"I sometimes wonder if I'm cut out to be a Spider Rider at all," Hunter confided.

Corona looked shocked. "Of course, you're cut out to be a Spider Rider, Hunter Steele," she said. "You would not wear the manacle if you were not suited to do so. Besides, you've helped us countless times since you first came to our world. And…" She paused to gaze into his eyes.

"And…?" he asked, feeling a bit wary.

Corona swallowed to clear her throat. "And you are an Earthen," she said. "Your coming heralds the great battle between Turandot and Insector."

"And that's a good thing? I don't know, Corona, sometimes I just feel like baggage here—or worse, bait. I mean, Lumen sent us out just to attract Stags into the open."

"That was not the only reason," Corona said, "but it was part of the plan. What of it, though? Who would you have go in your stead? Me? I would gladly have gone if asked."

Hunter flushed. "No. That's not what I meant at all."

A thought from Shadow appeared in Hunter's mind. "Not doing a great job expressing yourself here, are you?"

"Shut up!" Hunter thought back. The last thing he needed at the moment was a surly spider distracting him.

"What I mean," Hunter continued, "is that if somebody's sending me into a trap, I'd at least like to know about it beforehand."

Shadow's voice appeared again. "Venus says that Magma didn't know either—nor did the legion. Only Igneous and Corona knew."

"Shadow is right," Corona said. Either Venus had passed along Shadow's comment, or Shadow had been mind-talking loud enough for Corona to hear.

Despite the progress he'd made, Hunter wished he were better at mind talk. "Well, that just makes my point, doesn't it," he said aloud. "Keeping us in the dark could have gotten someone killed."

"Someone like you?" Shadow added sarcastically.

"Shut up!" Hunter thought back again.

"But no one got killed," Corona said. "Everything turned out according to plan. And the reason only Igneous and I were told is because keeping the mission's true nature secret was essential. The Oracle fears we may be going up against a telepathic power nearly as strong as she."

"Really?" Hunter asked, feeling a bit worried now.

"Yes," Corona replied. "Igneous says that the Oracle's scans to locate the exact position of the next shard have been blocked—only a powerful telepath could do that."

Another voice appeared in Hunter's head, the gentle voice of Corona's spider, Venus. "The Oracle kept the mission secret for your own protection," she said.

Hunter nodded. "I remember. Stray thoughts…"

"Exactly," Venus replied.

"What about now?" Hunter asked, worrying that his mind still might not be strong enough to prevent errant thoughts.

"Now we have the decoys returning to the city," Corona said. "We hope that will confuse the Insector spies, both physical and telepathic."

Hunter nodded.

"I'll help you block stray thoughts as well," Shadow said. Shadow seemed edgy to Hunter, though he couldn't figure out why.

They ate and slept and ate again before they descended from the highlands to the rolling coastline of the Great Sea.

As they drew near the huge body of water, Shadow's apprehension grew.

"Ask Igneous if we're going to build rafts to float across," Shadow said.

"Why don't you ask Flame?" Hunter mind-talked back.

"I don't want to appear foolish to the other spiders," Shadow said.

"Oh, and it's okay if I look like an idiot to the other riders," Hunter said.

"Well, it's something you're used to, anyway," Shadow replied.

"Har-de-har-har," said Hunter. He turned to Corona. "Are we going to make a raft to cross the sea?" he asked.

"That would be too slow," Corona said. "We'll swim across on spiderback."

Hunter nodded. The plan made sense; the air pockets in a spider's hairs made it naturally buoyant. But immediately after he thought it, Hunter's heart nearly froze with fear.

It took him a moment to realize that the fear he felt was coming not from himself but from Shadow.

"Shadow!" Hunter thought urgently, trying to shield his thoughts from the others as best he could. "What's wrong? Are we under attack, or…?"

A long, empty silence hung in the humid air. Finally, the spider replied.

"I can't swim!"

11
Hydrophobia

"Um…" Hunter began, trying his utmost to be tactful with Shadow, "why can't you swim?"

"I've never learned how!" Shadow replied.

Hunter had met people who couldn't swim. Usually, they were kids from the city who'd never lived near a swimming pool or a pond or the ocean. Hunter had been one of those kids until his family moved to the countryside. But he'd never heard of an animal that couldn't swim.

"It's easy," he told Shadow via mind talk. "You probably know how instinctively."

"Well, what if I don't?" Shadow shot back. "How can we know? I've never tried it before!"

Corona looked toward the two of them, concerned. "Is something wrong?" she asked.

"Nothing," Hunter replied.

Corona looked as though she didn't believe him. "Venus thought she heard you and Shadow arguing."

"It's nothing," Hunter snapped. "Just guy stuff. We're working on shielding our thoughts."

"Well, work at it harder," Venus's pleasant voice suggested.

"Yeah. Okay," Hunter told her. He turned his thoughts back to Shadow. "I can't believe you'd face down a hundred crazed Centipedians but be afraid of a little water," he said.

"It's not a little water," Shadow replied. "It's *a lot* of water—so much water that you can't see the bottom!"

In Hunter's mind, an image formed of Shadow getting water in his many eyes and his breathing orifices. He felt the spider's mounting panic.

"The bottom only matters if you sink, and you're not going to sink," Hunter thought back. "You've crossed rivers, haven't you?"

"Yes, but I could always touch then or at least see the other side," Shadow thought. "This ocean is too big. I will drown for sure, and I'll probably drag you down with me."

"No you won't," Hunter said firmly.

"How do you know?"

"I know because, for one thing, I'm a very good swimmer," he said. "Besides, you're *not* going to sink. Spiders are naturally buoyant."

"That's what you say," Shadow countered. "But I've seen humans sink, and you're a lot smaller and lighter than an armored battle spider."

"I doubt we'll be using our armor during the crossing," Hunter said. Then he turned to Corona and asked aloud, "Will we be swimming across the ocean in our battle armor?"

"Of course not," she replied. "We don't want to use manacle power if we can help it. We need to save that energy to rescue the shard. That's one reason Lumen and the Oracle set up the elaborate decoy scheme."

"Yeah. That makes sense," Hunter said. Then, to Shadow, he added, "See? There's nothing to worry about."

"What do you mean?" Shadow thought. "I still have everything to worry about that I had a moment ago!"

Hunter felt a bit exasperated. "Look," he said, "I didn't always know how to swim, either." He concentrated hard, not wanting any of the other spiders or their riders to overhear his mind talk. "In fact, other kids used to tease me about it."

"Really?" Shadow asked. Hunter felt a bit of the spider's fear slipping away.

"Sure," Hunter replied. "They used to tease me all the time. Sometimes, they'd steal my hat and throw it into the neighbor's pool—just because they knew I wouldn't be able to retrieve it."

"Humans can be cruel," Shadow thought.

"Yeah? Well, life's tough whether you live on the earth or under it," Hunter said. "Anyway, I got really mad at those kids, and I decided to become a great swimmer."

"And you did?"

"Not at first—I was too scared. But one day my dad took me to my aunt's pool and just threw me into the deep end."

"That seems a bit cruel!" Shadow said, concerned.

"I learned to swim, no problem," Hunter replied. "Though I did have a little trouble getting out of the burlap bag!"

For a moment, Shadow seemed puzzled. Then he laughed. Hunter laughed as well.

"So…" Shadow said, "that story was a joke? Was any of it true?"

"You bet," Hunter replied. "The part about me teaching myself to swim is true. You can teach yourself, too. I know you can."

"But I don't have time to learn or practice before we get to Quagmiro," Shadow said.

85

"Look," Hunter replied, feeling a bit exasperated, "every animal I've ever seen knows how to swim—just by instinct. Besides, I'm a really good swimmer. I'll walk, er, swim you through it. We'll be fine just as long as we work together. Do you trust me?"

"Mostly."

"Okay, then trust me now," Hunter said firmly.

Shadow nodded his agreement, and the two of them followed the others down the shore and into the lapping green waters of the Great Sea.

Deep in the swamps of Quagmiro, Fungus Brain concentrated. Born from the stagnant water of Quagmiro, Fungus Brain had grown from one very intelligent cell—a fungus cell, true, but one that was nearly pure intellect. Now Fungus Brain controlled all in the swamp with great mental power.

Far away, a part of Fungus Brain lived in the palace of Mantid, the Insector leader. Fungus Brain was Mantid's newest ally. Fungus Brain's telepathy was very powerful. He could sense that disjointed part of himself if he concentrated on it, and—even without concentrating—he could tell when Mantid wanted to speak to him.

"What may we do for you, great Mantid?" Fungus Brain asked as an image of the Insector leader formed in his mind.

"My spies report that the Spider Riders will not reach Quagmiro," Mantid replied. "They were met en route by an Insector force led by my general Stags."

Fungus Brain burbled and hissed, not sure whether to be pleased or displeased by this news. "So, your Stags has...destroyed them?"

Even hidden behind his robes and impenetrable armor, Mantid seemed uncomfortable. "It's too early to tell," he said. "Indications are that the riders have returned to Arachnia."

"So, your Stags didn't slay them?" Fungus Brain said, trying not to let the delight show in his malevolent voice.

Mantid remained silent.

Fungus hissed gleefully. "We would guess you need a new member of the Big Four, O great Mantid."

"Does your telepathy tell you that?" Mantid asked. His voice remained cold and emotionless.

"We don't need telepathy to know that if the Spider Riders remain alive to return to their city, then Stags will not be returning to the land of the Insectors."

Mantid's voice grew even colder. "Protect the shard," he said. "Though Stags may have turned back the Spider Riders, they will surely attempt to reach Quagmiro again."

"We most assuredly hope so," Fungus Brain replied. He let his concentration lapse, and the image of Mantid faded away.

Fungus Brain turned to the dragonfly warrior standing beside him. The look of dull servitude on the warrior's face did not change as Fungus Brain spoke to the creature telepathically.

"Lord Mantid is a fool," Fungus Brain said, his thoughts the only thing in the dragonfly warrior's head, "and his underlings are incompetent."

"Why is that, master?" the dragonfly warrior asked. He spoke stiffly, compelled to do so by Fungus Brain's mesmerizing mental powers.

"Glad I had you ask that question. Why does Stags not pursue the Spider Riders?" Fungus Brain said. "Clearly, he has been defeated, possibly slain. And if Stags is defeated, why do the riders return to the city?"

"Perhaps they are injured. Perhaps they need to rest for the next battle," the dragonfly warrior suggested. "Perhaps they fear your greatness."

"I couldn't have said it better myself," Fungus Brain replied.

Fungus Brain thought a moment, his tendrils whirling agitatedly around his immense, flabby brain. "But the Spider Riders have never shown fear before—though we are far more worthy of fear than their usual Insector foes."

The dragonfly warrior didn't answer, so Fungus Brain compelled him to nod his agreement.

"Since Lord Mantid was wrong about his agent Stags, we are inclined to believe that he may be wrong about other things," Fungus Brain said. "He is certainly wrong in his estimation of his foes. How else would they defeat his plans so often? Therefore, he may be wrong that the Spider Riders have turned back. In fact, we doubt very much that they have given up so easily."

"What do you intend to do, Your Magnificence?" the dragonfly warrior droned.

"We shall ready our squadron of Water Strykers to defend Quagmiro," Fungus Brain said, sounding quite pleased with himself. "We shall array them in the ocean between Quagmiro and the mainland. Then we shall use our telepathy to probe the waters surrounding our kingdom. When we find the Spider Riders, we will send the Strykers to destroy them."

The huge, flabby creature chuckled until the drool falling from his maw formed a steaming pool at the base of his throne. "The spiders will be out of their element on the water," he said, "whereas our Strykers shall be right at home." A wicked gleam burned within his cruel eyes. "The Spider Riders shall drown in a sea of their own blood. And any who survive shall be dragged to our court to serve us...forever!"

12
Death on the Water

"This isn't so bad," thought Shadow as he paddled through the blue seawater. "I think I might survive this after all."

"I knew you would," Hunter said, trying to shield any lingering doubts he felt from his arachnid companion.

When they'd first hit the water, Shadow had seemed tentative and awkward. Venus, Brutus, and Flame adapted instantly—clearly, they'd been on ocean missions before.

Hunter urged Shadow on, though, and by watching the other spiders, the huge black arachnid soon got the hang of swimming.

Initially, he could manage only a tentative dog paddle—or "spider splash," as Hunter thought of it. Soon, however, Shadow gained a confident stride and swam much like the other spiders, if not quite as gracefully.

Hunter wondered if perhaps Venus was giving Shadow telepathic lessons, too. If so, Shadow had been very careful to shield those messages from Hunter.

The great spider's bulk heaved through the placid blue ocean. Hunter felt glad that they'd lucked into such a nice day for their "swimming lesson." He wasn't sure that even he, as good a swimmer as he was, would have felt confident during one of the fierce thunderstorms that often swept through the Inner World.

Gazing out to the curving horizon, Hunter saw storm clouds forming in the distance. "That's the direction of Mantid's fortress," he thought, "where the final shard is hidden. I'm going to find that shard. I'll do whatever it takes. I'll save Petra, if it's the last thing I do."

"Let's hope it's not!" Shadow interjected.

Hunter laughed. "Don't tell me you've grown accustomed to my face!" he said.

"We just work well together," Shadow thought. "It's not as if I'm attached to you or anything. Besides, if you get killed trying to help Petra, how are you going to reach the surface world again?"

"You've seen that in my mind?" Hunter asked. He felt annoyed that Shadow knew his secret desire. He'd been trying hard to keep it hidden.

"I see a lot when you're not paying attention," Shadow replied.

In his most shielded thought, Hunter reminded himself to constantly be on his mental guard. "And you're not upset that I'd like to return home?" he asked Shadow.

"Why should I be?" the spider responded. "My home is a web long tattered by time. A father I never knew. A mother who would eat her young if they didn't leave the web the day they were hatched. I'd like to see your home, though it sounds like a very strange place."

Hunter shook his head. "No," he said, laughing. "My home seems very normal. It's *this* place that's strange."

"Not to me," Shadow said. "Or to the others."

Hunter gazed across the short span of water separating them from the other Spider Riders. Corona, Igneous,

Magma, and their spiders were surging through the waves. Not one showed the slightest fear or trepidation.

"They're cut out to be Spider Riders," Shadow interjected. "Not like you and me. We're both loners at heart."

"Yeah," Hunter thought, "but I guess we're stuck being loners together."

"It could be worse," the spider replied.

Hunter nodded. It certainly could have been worse. At least he'd gotten over his fear of giant spiders. At least he and Shadow had formed a friendly partnership. At least as a Spider Rider he had a chance to help Petra. At least if he became an Arachna-Master, he had a chance—however slim—to return home someday.

"There it is," Corona said, pointing to a quivering land mass emerging from the sea mist. "Quagmiro."

Magma gazed at the overgrown, swampy shores. "It looks like a dump," he said.

"Dump or not," Igneous said, "that is where our goal lies. Pick up the pace. We want to get there before we're detected."

Shadow and the other spiders began swimming faster. They kicked up huge blue-green sprays of water into the humid air.

Hunter patted Shadow on the back. "You're doing great," he said.

"Quiet!" Shadow countered. "I'm trying not to think about it!"

Hunter chuckled. Then he spotted what looked like a geyser breaking the surface of the water between them and the shores of Quagmiro. First one geyser appeared, then two, then a half dozen, then more. They stitched their way across the surface of the water toward the Spider Riders.

The spouts seemed familiar to Hunter. "Are there whales in this ocean?" he asked aloud.

"Break formation!" Igneous commanded, both audibly and telepathically. "We've been spotted!"

Hotarla stumbled for about the hundredth time. She and the princess lurched sideways and crashed into a large, rough boulder.

"Ouch!" Sparkle cried. "Watch where you're going!"

"I would if I could!" Hotarla protested. "Why don't you turn off the invisibility power for a while?"

The princess sighed. "I know it's hard to walk while invisible," she said. "I'm having trouble, too. But that's no reason to give up."

"You can't find the right button, can you?" Hotarla thought darkly.

The princess didn't reply.

"I knew it!" the spider said. "You can't find the buttons to deactivate the power...again! What's that, the third time in as many tries?"

"I *can* find it," the princess replied hotly. "I mean, I *will*, once we've had enough practice."

"You should have practiced turning off the power more *before* we left the city," Hotarla thought back. "You should have practiced more before we got lost in this forsaken desert!"

"We're not lost," Sparkle replied. "How can we be lost? I can still see the castle."

"They can't see us, though, can they?" Hotarla thought. "If we were to fall into a crevasse or something, they might never find us!"

"They'd find us when our manacle power ran out," Sparkle said.

"Is that how you're planning to become visible again?" Hotarla asked. "By letting your manacle power run out, like last time?"

"No," Sparkle replied peevishly. She ran her fingers over the manacle's surface and pressed a series of studs. She and Hotarla became visible again.

"See?" Sparkle said. "I told you I knew what I was doing."

Hotarla sulked.

"Do you want to be a Spider Rider pair?" the princess asked.

"Of course!" the spider replied.

"Then you need to stop complaining so much," Sparkle said. "If we're ever to join the corps, we need to train more."

"But it's hard!" Hotarla complained. "My joints ache, and I'm tired all the time!"

"Me, too!" Sparkle countered. "But that's how we'll get stronger."

"By hurting?" Hotarla asked miserably.

"By concentrating on our goals even if it hurts," Sparkle said. "You don't see Flame or Brutus complaining, do you?"

"They're much bigger and stronger than I am," Hotarla thought.

"And they got bigger and stronger by training," the princess insisted. "Do you think either of them or Venus or Shadow got stronger by giving up?"

"I suppose not," Hotarla admitted.

"Then we won't give up, either," Sparkle said. "Come on. I'm going to make us invisible again. We'll keep training until

Lumen and the rest *can't* ignore us. We'll keep training until we become full-fledged Spider Riders!"

"Everyone scatter! Evasive maneuvers!" Igneous ordered.

The spiders did as they were told, immediately swimming off in four different directions.

"Incoming!" cried Magma.

As he spoke, a series of projectiles slammed into the water near Hunter and Shadow. The shots sent up huge spouts of spray—the same spray that Hunter had seen earlier. It didn't look like whale spouts, now, though, it looked like machine-gun fire.

"Where's it coming from?" Hunter wondered as Shadow zigged and zagged, trying to keep out of the way.

Just then, a hundred giant insects appeared out of the mist near the shores of Quagmiro. They skimmed along the surface of the water, their long legs outstretched. The short wings on their backs beat furiously, propelling them forward. The creatures had long, spikelike noses. Each nose spat a barrage of deadly spines toward the Spider Riders.

Corona's voice echoed across the telepathic link. "Water Strykers!"

"Everyone, armor up!" Igneous ordered.

All four riders immediately said, "Arachna might!" and activated their manacles. Their armor quickly formed around their bodies. Three of the spiders immediately went into battle mode as well, but not Shadow.

"I'll sink!" he thought desperately.

"Nobody else is sinking," Hunter thought back. "You can do it! We need the protection from those spikes the bugs are firing."

"It won't do any good," Shadow thought back. "Those skeleton spikes are super hard—just like our exoskeleton. They can penetrate even the toughest battle armor!"

"Not as easily as they can penetrate your regular armor!" Venus put in.

"We should stay mobile," Shadow thought desperately. "We're harder to hit that way."

"Do what Igneous said!" Hunter thought. "Change to battle mode now!"

Reluctantly, Shadow initiated the change that transformed his hair, spines, and chitinous skin into thick battle armor. As the armor formed around him, he slowed noticeably in the water, bobbed, and nearly went under.

"Concentrate!" Hunter thought. "You can do it!" He felt the spider's panic rising and tried to send positive thoughts along the mental link they shared. "If you lose it now, we are going to die a dozen different ways before we know it!"

"Oh, that's very comforting!" Shadow thought back sarcastically.

"Follow my lead!" Igneous called.

The other spiders swerved back into formation, heading straight for the front of the Water Stryker column. Most of them deftly dodged the barrage of incoming barbs shot their way.

One spike skidded off the side of Shadow's armor. "Ouch!" the spider thought.

"Concentrate!" Hunter said.

"You telling me to concentrate is like Magma telling me to stay cool!" Shadow thought back.

The Water Strykers swarmed straight ahead, looking to overwhelm the spiders by sheer numbers.

Just as it seemed the two forces would crash directly into each other, Igneous called, "Break!"

By telepathic agreement, Shadow and Brutus split left, while Venus and Flame split right. They swerved wide and then turned, catching the column of Strykers between them.

"Fire!" Igneous cried.

Hunter let loose with stun blasts from his manacle, knocking out a half dozen Strykers in as many seconds. Shadow fired sleep darts, felling as many more in the same time.

Igneous and Corona used similar tactics, though their experience allowed them to land their blows more expertly. With every charge fired they knocked one Stryker into the one next to it, thereby doubling the effect of their stun blasts.

Magma did even better. For each expertly timed blast from his manacle, he stunned three of the enemy, and Brutus felled three more with sleep darts.

The edges of the Stryker formation lost cohesion. They panicked, forgetting to fire their deadly spikes. Only the forward motion of the group kept the enemy bugs together. By the time they sped past the Spider Rider attack formation, a full seventy-five Strykers lay unconscious in the sea. The Insectors' sports car–size bodies floated like fallen tree trunks in the green water and drifted lazily toward the shores of Quagmiro.

Hunter and the other riders re-formed as the Strykers sped past. Magma laughed. "Those bugs may be fast," he said, "but they're not too bright."

"There's enough of them that they don't have to be bright," Igneous reminded him.

"Don't let your guard down," Corona agreed.

97

"Let's keep heading for shore," Hunter suggested. "They lose their advantage if we reach land."

"The kid's right," Magma said.

"Agreed," said Igneous. "Keep moving. When they swing around to get us, we'll split again and spin on them."

The other riders and their spiders telepathically agreed to the plan and struck out for shore once again. The spiders moved less quickly in their armor, and Shadow had trouble keeping his head above water.

"Don't panic!" Hunter thought. "You'll be okay."

"Easy for you to say!" Shadow puffed, struggling.

"You can do it, Shadow," Venus urged.

"We know you can," added Corona.

Slowly, the armored spiders and their riders swam through the stunned Strykers toward the distant shore.

As they did, the remaining swarm of Strykers executed a long, looping turn for another attack run.

"Here they come again!" Magma warned.

13
Strykers from the Sea

The Strykers came in fast and hard. This time, though, they were coming from behind the Spider Riders, rather than meeting them head-on.

"Split up!" Igneous ordered telepathically. "Four directions. Keep heading for shore."

The spiders immediately did as he commanded, but the Strykers seemed ready for that maneuver. As the riders split, the Strykers broke into four smaller groups, one chasing each spider.

The Strykers fired their skeleton spikes, but the spiders' multiple eyes alerted them to the threat. They dodged the missiles as best they could, despite being slowed by their armor.

One spike bounced off Hunter's arm, right next to his manacle. He winced in pain, but neither the bracelet nor his armor seemed damaged.

"Spin and attack!" Igneous ordered.

Instantly, all four spiders whirled in place, firing stun darts. More Strykers splashed into the water, unconscious.

"I'll do better this time," Hunter thought, trying to imitate the firing pattern of the others.

His first stun bolt caused one Stryker to crash into another. His second clipped one, barely, but still knocked it out. His third bolt, though, missed entirely.

"Don't get fancy," Shadow thought. "Stick to tactics you know."

"I'm still breaking even—three shots, three stuns," Hunter replied, feeling slightly annoyed with himself for not doing better.

A Stryker veered right at them. Hunter ducked as the Insector fired a skeleton spike at his head.

"Shield!" Shadow warned.

Hunter activated his manacle's power shield and turned. He barely got the shield in front of the Stryker's pointed nose as it tried to skewer him. The impact rocked him in his seat, but he stayed aboard Shadow's back.

Shadow whirled, grabbed the Insector in his mandibles, and flung it aside. The huge bug hit the water and skidded across the surface, out cold. "Pay attention!" Shadow snapped.

Hunter knew the spider was worried—both about Hunter and about his own ability to fight in the water while wearing battle armor.

"Form up!" Igneous's telepathic command echoed in their minds. "We've lost the element of surprise," the Spider Rider commander said. "Close in! We'll have to fight back-to-back."

Shadow and Hunter charged into the mass of Water Strykers separating them from the other spiders while Corona, Igneous, and Magma did the same.

Skeleton spikes sprayed around them in a deadly barrage. Hunter fended off dozens of spines with his shield as he and Shadow moved toward their comrades, but they didn't have time to fire any stun bolts.

Shadow shot as many stun darts as he could and knocked more opponents out of their way with his legs and mandibles. "I am really hating this!" Shadow thought.

"You're doing great!" Hunter replied, wishing his own tactics had been as effective.

The four Spider Riders met up amid a sea of floating, stunned Strykers.

"Back-to-back now," Igneous said. "Protect one another and watch for openings. When we've thinned them out sufficiently, we'll make a break for shore."

The others did as he commanded. The spiders positioned themselves tail to tail, each one facing a point of the compass.

Hunter gazed out over the sea of Strykers swarming in toward them and wondered if Igneous's plan had any chance of success.

"Fire at will!" Igneous commanded.

The riders all powered up their stun blasts and raked the incoming Strykers. At the same time, they used their shields to protect themselves and the rest of the group from the Insectors' skeleton spikes.

Strykers fell in great waves. Their bodies piled up around the Spider Riders, offering some protection from the next wave of attackers. The Insectors kept coming, though, trying to fire their spikes through their downed fellows and into the enemy. Hunter's arms began to feel leaden from deflecting shots.

"Don't think about it," Shadow counseled. "Keep fighting!"

Hunter blinked the sweat out of his eyes and replied, "As if I have a choice!"

Magma must have overheard their mind talk, because the big Turandot laughed. As he did, a barrage of skeleton spikes raked toward him and Brutus. The two of them fended off a dozen barbs, but even the experienced rider and his spider could not defend everywhere at once.

Magma bellowed as a spike pierced his armor and bit into his shoulder. He lost his balance and toppled into the water. The big Turandot went under, but his armor's automatic protection systems kicked in. The breathing mask covered his face, and a few seconds after he'd sunk, he bobbed to the surface once more.

"Magma's been hit!" Hunter cried.

"We all know that!" Shadow said. "Watch yourself."

Hunter turned and knocked aside a spike with his shield as Magma swam weakly back toward Brutus. "Brutus is hit, too!" he called. "I'm all right! Defend! Defend!"

The big spider wobbled uneasily, several spikes protruding from his armored carapace. The Strykers swarmed in, trying to take advantage of the Spider Riders' weakness.

"Cover Brutus's quadrant," Igneous commanded, though Hunter and Corona had already moved to do so. "Forget the stun blasts. Use your full powers!"

"But our manacle energy—" Hunter protested.

"Won't do any good if we're all dead!" Igneous countered.

"Lightning lance!" Corona cried.

Scintillating power blasted forth from her armored hands. The electrical power arced through the ranks of Strykers and shorted through the seawater, knocking out a huge swath of the enemy.

"Good thing she knew where to place that blast," Hunter thought, "or all of us would have been fried."

"Corona knows what she's doing," Shadow replied. "Just make sure you do."

Hunter nodded and said, "Sonic charge!"

He let rip with as powerful a blast as he could. The ocean in front of him shuddered with the force of the concussion. A huge wave of sound-propelled water swept the Strykers back, away from the beleaguered Spider Riders.

At the same time, Igneous let loose with a spectacular fire bolt. The ocean in front of him exploded and burst into clouds of hot steam. Strykers flew through the air and crashed into the surf. They didn't get back up.

"Nice display," Magma said through gritted teeth, "too bad we can't keep it up forever." He smiled, though it was obvious to everyone that both he and Brutus were in serious pain.

"Plasma burst!" Magma grunted. He sprayed a wide blast across the ocean, and many of the Strykers that remained toppled into the waves. The remaining Insectors buzzed around, confused.

"We've thinned the ranks," Corona said, "but there are still too many of them."

"If only we could use our webs!" Shadow thought. "But our spinnerets are all submerged."

"Wait! That's it!" Hunter said.

"What's what?" Shadow asked.

"You can use your webs!"

"But I just told you—"

"No," Hunter said. "I mean you can get out of the water and use your webs."

Shadow looked around. "In case you hadn't noticed, we're in the middle of the ocean."

"You'll have to climb on top of the other spiders' backs," Hunter said.

"But that's crazy," Shadow replied. "We'll all sink!"

"No you won't," Hunter said. "All of you spiders have buoyancy to spare—which is how you can carry us humans while you swim."

"You weigh a lot less than I do, Hunter," Shadow said.

"I'm telling you, you can do it!" Hunter replied.

"Venus and the others agree," Corona put in. She and her spider had apparently been listening in.

"But I can't!" Shadow pleaded.

"The Strykers are getting back into formation," Hunter warned.

Just out of dart range, the Water Stryker swarm gathered into a coherent group once more. They swung around toward the weary Spider Riders.

"Do it now!" Igneous ordered.

The Strykers sped forward.

Shadow lifted his front legs and placed them on Venus's back. All the spiders were slick with water, and Shadow had trouble getting his grip.

He lurched up and onto the edge of the "platform" made from the bodies of the other three spiders. The spiders sank a bit, and they wobbled terribly, but—just as Hunter had guessed—they supported Shadow's and Hunter's weight.

"Just a little farther!" Hunter thought. "We need to get your whole body out of the water!"

"I'm trying!" Shadow replied.

The Strykers fired their skeleton spikes as they raced in.

"Defensive blasts! Full power!" Igneous commanded.

Hunter and the other Spider Riders responded with blasts of sound, flame, plasma, and lightning. They scorched the spines from the air, and the missiles fell harmlessly into the sea. The Stryker swarm kept coming and kept firing, too.

"Shields!" Igneous said. "Protect Hunter and Shadow so they can get into position!"

Shadow lurched forward onto the makeshift sea platform. The other spiders tried to help, but they were none too stable bobbing amid the waves.

Hunter glanced at his power manacle. Already the warning gem was flashing. "We're almost out of power, and we haven't even reached Quagmiro!" he thought.

With one final, great heave, Shadow righted himself on the other spiders' backs. He spun to face the incoming enemy swarm—and nearly lost his footing.

"Careful!" Magma cautioned.

"I'm trying!" Shadow thought back.

The Stryker formation sped toward them, filling the air with a deadly barrage.

Shadow aimed his spinnerets.

"Now!" Igneous cried.

As the Insectors came within range, Shadow fired every ounce of web that he could.

The webbing spread out in a huge capture net. The Strykers sped headlong into it, firing as they came.

Several spikes got through the Spider Riders' guard and hit Brutus.

The big spider wobbled precariously, and Shadow lost his footing.

Shadow and Hunter pitched headfirst off the makeshift platform, crashed into the water, and sank.

14
Depths of Fear

The blue-green water quickly turned black as Hunter and Shadow sank into the depths.

The breathing equipment in Hunter's armor automatically covered his face. After a moment, he could see and breathe again.

"Shadow, what are you doing?" he thought in mind talk.

"I'm sinking!" Shadow cried.

"Well, I can see that," Hunter thought back. "But why?"

"Because I'm too heavy!" Shadow replied.

"No you're not," Hunter said. "You're panicking! Stop it!"

"Easy for you to say!"

Hunter forced himself to remain calm. "You were swimming just a few minutes ago," he said. "You can swim now, too. You swim like a fish!"

"And sink like a stone!" Shadow wailed plaintively.

"Look," Hunter said, "spiders have air trapped within their body hairs. That's how you and the others can float in the first place, even in full armor. If you stop thrashing around, you'll surface in no time."

Hunter felt his friend's panic subsiding. "C'mon!" he thought. "The others may need our help!"

With two quick sweeps of his huge legs, Shadow propelled them back to the surface.

They pushed past the bodies of hundreds of stunned Strykers and found their friends nearby. The Spider Riders were battered and tired, but they were all in one piece. The greater mass of the Stryker swarm floated nearby, entangled in Shadow's huge web. Those still free were rapidly skimming away from the battle. The Spider Riders had won!

Igneous spotted Hunter and Shadow and waved them back to the group. "What took you so long?" he asked. "We could have used your help."

"We got caught in some seaweed when we went under," Hunter said to protect Shadow.

"Thanks," Shadow thought quietly to him.

"How is everybody?" Hunter asked.

"I've been better," Magma groaned.

"We can't tend your wounds here," Corona said. "And even if we could, we don't want to remain in the open."

"Right," Igneous agreed. "Everyone swim to shore as quickly as you can."

None of them needed to hear that command twice. The battle spiders all swam for the swampy landmass nearby. Brutus lagged behind a bit, but Shadow, Venus, and Flame helped him along.

By the time they reached the shores of Quagmiro, the entire group was sweaty and exhausted.

They pulled themselves up on the boggy sod that served as the island's shoreline. The shore heaved and wobbled, as though floating on the surface of the sea.

Magma, barely clinging to Brutus's back, looked around and grunted, "What a dump!"

The mire stretched for miles in every direction: bog, peat, and twisted trees hung with moss. Fog and drizzle filled the hot, stagnant air. In the distance a low mountain loomed at the island's center.

"There's no place to make camp here," Corona noted. "We should move under the trees, out of sight of the shore, and then tend our wounds."

Igneous nodded his agreement. Spiders and riders slogged through the muck and into the moss-draped forest. As they rode, the sky opened up with a torrent of rain.

"Just what I needed," Magma said, "a nice shower." Despite his bravado, his words came out faint and slurred.

"He's going to pass out if we go much farther without getting those spikes out," Corona said.

"We'll stop here, then," Igneous ordered. He raised his hand, and the whole group came to a stop.

Hunter and Shadow leaned against a big tree while Corona and Igneous looked at Magma's and Brutus's wounds.

Hunter peered through the mist and into the tangled swamp. There didn't seem to be any dry land at all. "Nice vacation spot," he said.

"Not the kind of place I intend to retire to," Shadow agreed.

Hunter winced at a shot of pain, then realized it wasn't his own. "Shadow, are you all right?" he asked. "Did you get hit by one of those spikes?"

"Grazed by a couple, but I'm okay," Shadow replied. "I'm just feeling a little stiff."

"Not as stiff as Magma and Brutus, I bet," Hunter said. He and Shadow glanced toward their wounded friends.

"We can't get these spikes out while they're in battle mode," Igneous said to Corona.

Corona nodded her agreement. "Yes. We'll have to use our energy knives to cut them out."

"Are you—ugh!—sure that's necessary?" Magma asked. He could barely speak through his clenched teeth, but his eyes remained brave.

"Well, we could just leave the spines in until they get infected and kill you," Corona replied.

"Brutus and I...will pass on that," Magma said.

With a burst of energy and a grunt of pain, he and his spider transformed out of their armor and into pedestrian mode. Without the armor, the sharp spikes sticking into Magma and Brutus were easily visible.

Hunter winced; he hadn't seen wounds that nasty in a rider or spider before. Venus and Flame supported Brutus, so he wouldn't collapse into the mud. Magma nearly fell, but Corona caught him on the way down.

She hefted him up onto Brutus's back to start tending his wounds. "You're going to be all right," she said.

Magma cracked a pained half smile. "With you taking care of me, how could I not be?"

For some reason, Magma's words made Hunter feel tight across his chest.

"Are you all right?" Shadow asked.

"Sure," Hunter replied. "I must have just strained a muscle while we were fighting. Don't worry about it. I'll be fine."

"Corona," Igneous said, "you handle Brutus—you're better with spider healing than I am. I'll help Magma."

Corona nodded her agreement.

Magma moaned. "C'mon, Iggy, give me a break!" His eyes rolled back in their sockets. He looked dizzy and half conscious.

109

Igneous ignored the quip and gazed at Hunter. "You and Shadow scout the area. See what you can find. Make sure there are no more Insectors sneaking up on us. After you've secured the perimeter, set up a lookout post a few hundred yards away."

Hunter nodded. "Right."

"And be sure to stay alert," Igneous added.

"Right."

Hunter settled in on Shadow's back, and the two of them headed inland, toward the mist-shrouded uplands.

"'Stay alert'!" Hunter said in mind talk, imitating Igneous's voice. "What does he think I'm going to do, fall asleep while I'm supposed to be keeping watch?"

"I'm sure he's just nervous because we're trapped in a strange land with two wounded comrades and very little manacle power left," Shadow said.

"Is that what you're getting from Flame?" Hunter asked.

"No," the spider replied. "I was just trying to make you feel better."

Hunter chuckled softly. "Thanks."

The rain and fog pressed in around them, making it difficult to see the tortured landscape. Hunter and Shadow circled the camp but spotted no sign of any Insectors.

"Let's put our lookout post uphill," Hunter suggested. "It'll be easier to see enemies coming from both directions, that way. The ground will be dryer, too, which will help some. At least, it'll make the watching a bit more comfortable."

Shadow agreed and they slogged through the mire uphill several hundred yards. They soon arrived at a relatively dry spot with a good vantage point. They had a clear view down into the camp, though they were still well below the mountain summit. Hunter dismounted. "I'll watch uphill," he said. "You watch back toward the camp."

"Don't want to watch the surgery, eh?" Shadow said.

"Not particularly," Hunter replied.

"I don't blame you."

The two of them settled into watching, peering through the mist and rain, trying to spot any enemies that might sneak up on the main group. The downpour leaked into the seams of Hunter's armor, soaking him to the skin. He could have reactivated the armor's underwater seals, but he didn't think it wise to expend the manacle energy.

In a very short time, he felt cold, wet, and miserable. The fog pressing in all around made him feel very much alone.

"You are not alone," Shadow said quietly via mind talk. "You'll never be alone so long as we're together."

Hunter nodded. "Yeah. Thanks."

The spider mentally sighed.

"What?" Hunter asked.

"But we won't always be together," Shadow said.

"What do you mean?" Hunter asked. His stomach clenched with apprehension.

"As you get older, your telepathic powers will wane," Shadow said.

"You can't be sure of that," Hunter replied. "I'm Earthen, remember, not Turandot."

"But all Turandot were Earthen at one time," Shadow replied. "And all Turandot, when they grow up, lose their telepathic bond with their spiders."

"Well, I won't if I can help it," Hunter said.

The spider shook his great, armored head. "Don't worry about it," he said. "Every spider knows when he or she takes a rider that the time of separation will come."

An almost unbearable sadness welled up within Hunter. "A-and what will you do, then?"

"I'll do what every battle spider does."

"Which is…?"

"I'll retire."

A funny image popped into Hunter's head. He imagined Shadow, Brutus, Venus, and many other spiders lounging on a palm-dotted beach somewhere, sipping ice tea and talking about the grand adventures they'd had.

"Actually," Shadow said, reading his mind, "it *is* something like that."

"Really?" Hunter asked.

Hunter heard the spider's gentle laughter in his mind. "Well, a little bit, anyway," Shadow said. "When a rider retires and takes his second profession, a battle spider goes to the land of Valeria."

"Where's that?" Hunter asked.

"It's a lush valley far away," Shadow replied.

As he spoke, the spider's mental image of Valeria began to form in Hunter's mind. The boy had to admit, it didn't look bad.

"In Valeria," Shadow continued, "a spider can hunt at will. We return to our lives as they were before we became joined to our riders."

"Kind of like going back to your roots," Hunter said.

Shadow understood what he meant, if not Hunter's words, and nodded. "We spiders often talk of Valeria—of living without human laws and obligations."

"I'd like to do that myself, sometimes," Hunter said wryly.

"Alas, for humans, obligations only become greater as you grow older."

"Hey, cut that out," Hunter said. "I don't want to think about that. Besides, it'll be a long time before you and I have to split up. I'm pretty young, you know."

Shadow shook his immense head. "Not so young as you think," he said. "Already, you're growing up—and the time of our parting is not too far away." He shifted his huge, armored body and winced.

A stab of sympathetic pain shot through Hunter.

"Are you sure you're okay?" the boy asked.

"I'm fine," Shadow replied.

Hunter and the spider sat in the rain for a while, keeping their thoughts private.

Finally, Hunter said, "I bet Igneous didn't much like it when Magma called him Iggy." He smiled slightly and chuckled.

"Magma wasn't himself," Shadow said. "The wound was making him delirious."

"Yeah," Hunter said, "but I bet Igneous didn't like it."

"I'm sure he didn't," Shadow said.

"Igneous bugs me so much sometimes," Hunter griped. "Maybe I should call him Iggy, too."

"I wouldn't advise it," Shadow replied. "Unless you want to send me into early retirement. A spider retires if his rider is killed, too, you know."

Hunter swallowed hard. "Is…is that what will happen to Petra's spider if she doesn't recover?" he asked.

Shadow nodded.

Just then, a faint buzzing sound drifted to Hunter's ears.

"Insectors!" he hissed.

15
Mired in Quagmiro

Before Hunter could locate the source of the buzzing sound, a scream echoed up to them from below.

Hunter recognized the deep voice. "Magma!" he cried. Immediately, he dashed to mount Shadow's back.

"Hold on," the spider said. "There's nothing to worry about—Magma and the others are all right."

"But that scream..." Hunter said.

"Igneous is removing the spikes from Magma's body, remember?" Shadow said.

Hunter felt like a dope for forgetting.

"So, instead of worrying about that," Shadow said, "worry about the Insectors. And whatever you do, don't yell again!"

Again, Hunter felt like a dope. "Right," he thought back.

The buzzing sound had grown louder as they conversed, but neither of them saw any signs of Insectors approaching the Spider Rider camp below.

"They're overhead," Shadow thought. With his many eyes, he sometimes spotted things a human could not.

Hunter looked up and saw shadowy shapes darting through the murky sky, just below the rain clouds. He couldn't make out what kind of Insectors they might be.

"They're heading inland," he mind-talked, "toward the center of the island."

"Maybe whoever's got the shard is calling for reinforcements," Shadow said.

"Probably," Hunter replied. "After that sea battle, they'd have to be expecting us."

"It may work out yet," Shadow thought. "Igneous is a very clever leader—for a human."

"We need to tell him about the Insectors," Hunter thought.

"I'll open up a mind link to Flame," Shadow replied.

After a few moments, Shadow reported Igneous's orders: "Return here and form up. We're moving out."

Hunter mounted Shadow's back, and the two quickly rode down the soggy hill.

As they neared the bottom, Magma yelped again as Igneous pulled another spike from his side.

"Thank the Oracle that was the last one!" Magma said, gasping with relief.

Igneous activated his manacle's healing hand function. The power's blue aura quickly closed up Magma's wound. The big warrior still didn't look too steady, though. He leaned heavily against his spider.

Corona pulled one of the two remaining spines out of Brutus's heavy armor. Brutus didn't even flinch, but seeing it, Hunter did.

"If someone pulled a spike like that out of me," he thought to Shadow, "I'd probably yell louder than Magma did."

"You are not a battle spider," Shadow said. "In any case, let's hope we never have to find out how much you yell when pierced by an Insector spine."

"I'm with you on that," Hunter agreed. He got off the spider's back as Corona prepared to pull the final spike out of Brutus.

Hunter walked into the swampy forest at the edge of the camp.

"Are you all right?" Shadow asked.

"Just stretching my legs," Hunter said. He did a lunge on one leg just to make the point. Actually, he felt a bit queasy, though he didn't want to admit it to the spider.

"Don't want to see Corona remove the final spike, eh?" Shadow guessed. A faint, spidery chuckle echoed across the mind link.

"That's not it," Hunter replied hotly. He was glad that the others couldn't see his reaction. "I told you, I just need to stretch my—"

"Wait a minute," Shadow interrupted. "We…we're all shutting down mind talk."

Hunter felt as though a door had just slammed shut in his face. All of a sudden, the swamp seemed deadly quiet. Hunter froze, hidden from Shadow and the others by a stand of cypress trees. He felt more alone than he'd felt in ages.

"Shadow?" Hunter thought.

No reply.

"Shadow…?" he thought more urgently.

Nothing. Mind-numbing silence.

He ran back through the trees, calling aloud, "Shadow…?"

He almost ran smack into Igneous riding Flame. "Quiet!" the Spider Rider leader snapped aloud but at a hush, glowering at Hunter. "Do you want every Insector in the Inner World to hear you?"

Hunter felt both ashamed at being scolded and annoyed at Igneous's high-and-mighty attitude. "What's going on?" he whispered.

"Do as you're told! Stay off mind link!" Igneous whispered back. "The spiders have sensed some kind of mind probe. Someone, or some*thing*, is looking for us. Whatever it is, we don't want to be found—either by mind talk or the regular loud-mouthed novice warrior kind." He glared at Hunter again.

Hunter folded his arms and whispered harshly, "I wouldn't have shouted if someone bothered to keep me in the loop!"

"I don't know what this loop is, or why you want to be in it," Igneous said sternly, "but now is *not* the time! Mount up. We're leaving."

He and Flame wheeled away from Hunter and headed toward the island's interior. As Hunter climbed up on Shadow's back, Corona helped Magma aboard Brutus. Then the three of them followed after their leader.

Hunter and Shadow drew close to Corona as she rode. "How's Magma?" Hunter whispered.

"He's weak," she replied. "The healing hand power can seal wounds but not replace lost blood. Brutus is in better shape."

"Should Magma be moving at all, then?"

"We had to change location," Corona said, "in case the enemy telepath had a fix on us. We'll stop as soon as we're sure it's safe."

"Good," Hunter said. "All of us could use some rest."

Corona looked slightly puzzled. "We're not resting," she said. "Only Magma and Brutus are resting. The rest of us will continue with the mission, of course."

"But that's crazy," Hunter said. "We're down to three riders, and our manacle energy is almost gone. Whoever has this shard will be guarding it well. We'll need the whole squad to take it."

Igneous fell back beside them and said. "Attacking now will throw the enemy off guard. It's the last thing they'll expect."

"That's what you said about crossing the ocean, too," Hunter reminded him. "And we still got attacked by about a thousand Water Strykers."

"What's the matter, Earthen?" Igneous asked. "Did you use up all your courage in the last battle?"

Hunter turned slightly red. "That's not it, and you know it," he said. "But there's no sense in us all getting ourselves killed. Why don't we just wait until we're back at full strength?"

"We don't have time," Igneous replied. "The fact that the enemy hasn't attacked yet means he doesn't know where we are or what we're up to. Our best chance is to strike now, when he's not ready."

"But do you really think the six of us can do it?" Hunter said.

"No," Igneous replied, "I think the *four* of us can do it—you, me, Flame, and Shadow. Corona will be staying to tend Magma, while Venus distracts the enemy."

"How?" Hunter asked.

"She'll move up the coastline, sending out false telepathic messages," Corona explained.

"The enemy will home in on Venus, giving us time to rescue the shard," Igneous said.

"We hope," Corona concluded.

Hunter nodded. It seemed like a sound plan, though he didn't like splitting up the group in this strange country. "But won't the telepath sense the rest of us coming?" he asked.

"Not if we avoid mind talk," Igneous said. "Human minds are too weak for telepaths to lock onto. Whoever is Mantis's agent in this land was locking onto our spiders. But with mind talk shut down…" He smiled. "Well, I hope we'll have a good chance of catching him by surprise."

Igneous looked around. They'd come upslope quite a bit from their original camp and were riding through an overgrowth of bushy moss. "Corona, Magma, and Brutus can stop here," he said. "Venus knows what she has to do. Hunter, you and I will continue upslope, the direction those Insectors you saw were heading. In a dismal place like this, Flame's heat-sensing abilities should be able to locate the shard once we get close."

This was the first time Hunter had heard mention of Flame's heat-sensing power. He wanted to ask Shadow about it, but because mind talk was shut down, he couldn't.

Magma sat up straight as they stopped amid the mossy clearing. "Home already…?" he mumbled, and then slumped over once more.

Corona got off Venus's back and helped him down. "Mmm," Magma said, "solid ground." He closed his eyes and lay down amid the damp moss.

Igneous motioned uphill and said to Hunter, "Let's go."

Already, Venus had moved off to relay her false telepathic signals. If the Insectors attacked, would Brutus be enough to help Corona and the wounded Magma?

Hunter hoped so.

He took one last glance at Corona and the others, then turned uphill and focused on the task ahead.

The ground went steadily upward. As they rode, the rain died away, and the clinging mist began to thin as well. The shrub moss and tangled trees gave way to mossy ground cover and broken boulders.

Hunter knew that the Oracle had given Igneous some sense of where to look for the shard. Igneous had shared that information with Flame, who had shared it with the other spiders. Hunter hadn't thought to ask Shadow about it, though. He had assumed he'd be able to access the information when he needed it. But with mind talk shut down…

Hunter didn't like having to trust others to determine his fate. He liked to control his own destiny.

"Maybe that's why I have trouble with Igneous and Prince Lumen," he thought. "They're always telling me and the other Spider Riders what to do without explaining why. Corona is willing to take orders on faith. I haven't been a rider that long, though. I don't know them as well as she does. I wish I could talk to Shadow!"

Hunter took a deep breath and patted the gigantic spider on the back. A few of Shadow's six eyes looked back at him, but without telepathy, Hunter couldn't guess what the spider might be thinking.

"Hold," Igneous said quietly.

Hunter and Shadow stopped behind Igneous and Flame.

"What is it?" Hunter whispered.

Only a few yards remained between them and the top of the hill, but there was little cover. If they climbed up, they'd certainly risk being seen.

"One of us will have to chance a look," Igneous said.

SPIDER RIDERS

Hunter in Battle Mode

SPIDER RIDERS

Aqune in Pedestrian Mode

SPIDER RIDERS

Aqune in Battle Mode

SPIDER RIDERS

Hotarla in Pedestrian Mode

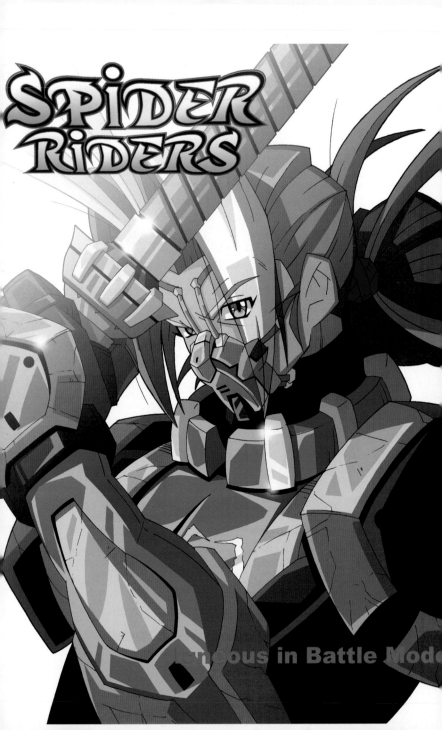

SPIDER RIDERS

A Centipedian

"I'll do it," Hunter offered, still stinging a bit from Igneous's earlier hint that he might be a coward.

The captain-general shook his head. "Flame will go," he said. "He moves more quickly than the rest of us, and his heat-sensing power will see through the darkness beyond the peak more clearly."

"Darkness?" Hunter asked. He hadn't been anywhere in the Inner World where the blazing core of the earth didn't shine. Even with the rain clouds, things never got really dark.

"The mountain is large enough to cast a shadow on the land beyond," Igneous explained. "Human eyes would take time to adjust, but Flame's ability goes beyond human sight. He'll be able to pick out the shard if it is nearby."

"Sounds like a plan," Hunter said.

Igneous looked puzzled. "Of course it's a plan," he said.

Hunter sighed. "That's an Earthen expression," he explained. "It means it sounds like a *good* plan."

Igneous frowned at him. "Then why didn't you just say that?"

As Flame scrambled up the rocky slope, Hunter, Igneous, and Shadow crouched low to the ground, trying to avoid being seen by any passing Insectors. The battle spider quickly reached the mountain's summit and peered into the shadowed land beyond.

After a moment, he crept backward and turned his head toward Igneous.

"Flame's found something," Igneous said.

"What?" Hunter asked.

Igneous scowled at him. "How would I know?" he said. "Mind talk is shut down. We'll have to see for ourselves."

16
Warriors' Square

Hunter, Shadow, and Igneous crept cautiously forward. They hadn't seen or heard any Insectors lately, but none of them was taking any chances. They used stray boulders and the billowing mist of the mountaintop as cover. When they reached the summit of the mountain, they used a small bit of manacle power to activate their armor's camouflage.

Downslope, the landscape quickly degenerated into moss and tangled trees once more. A vast swampland, similar to the one they'd slogged through, stretched away on the other side of the peak.

"Activate your distance viewer," Igneous commanded. "Scan pattern three."

Hunter did as he was told, and a small pair of magnifiers, like built-in binoculars, swung out of his visor and into place over his eyes. He scanned the landscape below, starting on his left and proceeding from near to far, as dictated in the pattern three protocols.

Before he had finished, though, Igneous tapped his shoulder. "There it is," the Spider Rider leader said softly. He pointed toward the bottom of the slope.

Hunter focused where Igneous indicated and saw a broad, flat marsh ringed by a stand of ancient cypresses. The trees looked to be at least a hundred feet tall. High above the swamp, the cypress branches intertwined, forming a dense green canopy. Drooping moss and long vines hung from the entangled branches.

The marsh was packed with Insectors, row after row of them aligned in a perfect square formation. The buglike warriors were tall, slender, and magnificently armored. Their two pairs of long wings lay folded flat against their backs. Their faces had large multifaceted eyes that seemed almost too big for their heads. Each of the warriors clutched a sawtooth spear; each had a curved sword strapped to its waist. Every Insector was facing out, away from the center of the clearing.

Hunter took a deep breath. There had to be at least two thousand of the bugs. "What are they?" he asked.

"Dragonfly warriors," Igneous replied. "I've faced them twice along the shores of the Great Sea. This must be where they come from. We never knew that before. Increase your magnification to twenty. We need to be sure of what they're guarding."

"Check," Hunter replied, and adjusted his viewer. He had to work a bit to see through the trees and around the many bodies of the dragonfly warriors. They stood very still, all their being focused on watching and guarding. As they shifted ever so slightly, something glittered in the darkness, and Hunter caught a glimpse of what they were protecting.

On a gnarled tree stump in the middle of the formation rested the seventh shard of the Oracle.

"That looks like the shard to me," Hunter said.

"To me as well," Igneous agreed. "That's what Flame saw, but we had to be sure. The Insectors are getting more clever, and it might have been some kind of trap."

"You mean more of a trap than having two thousand armed dragonfly warriors defending it?" Hunter asked.

"Yes," Igneous replied grimly.

"Um," Hunter began, "so what can these guys do, anyway?"

"They can fly and shoot dragon fire," Igneous said. "And of course they're lethal with their weapons as well."

Hunter frowned. "That's all?" he asked.

Igneous missed the sarcasm. "Yes," the Spider Rider leader replied.

"I don't suppose it matters that we're outnumbered five hundred to one," Hunter said.

"Of course it doesn't," Igneous said. "We're honor bound to retrieve that shard. Follow me, we're going in."

"Hang on a second. Don't we need a plan?"

"Surprise is our plan," Igneous said.

"And that's worked so well up to now."

"We're here, aren't we? And the shard is almost within our grasp."

"So, we're going to surprise these dragonflies by just rushing right in and fighting our way to the shard. Is that it?"

"That's it. We stun our way into the warriors' square using our swords and the spiders' darts and grab the shard. Do you have a problem with that?"

"It's not much of a plan," Hunter said.

Igneous reddened. "And you, the wet-behind-the-ears rider with the vast experience, have a better idea, I suppose," he said.

"As a matter of fact, I do," Hunter replied. He wished that he had Shadow's telepathic presence to back him up—or at least tell him he was out of his mind.

Igneous crossed his arms over his armored chest and looked skeptical. "Well…?" he said.

Hunter took a deep breath. "What you said about grabbing the shard gave me an idea. We don't want to just wade into that—what did you call it?—warriors' square. That's what they want us to do. That's what they're set up for."

"I know that," Igneous said, "but we're so low on manacle power and warriors that we have little choice. The Insectors have the shard well guarded on all four sides."

"*Four* sides," Hunter repeated. "That's just it. I don't suppose you've ever heard of Tarzan?"

"Tar's ant?" Igneous said, both puzzled and annoyed.

"Tarzan," Hunter said. "He's kind of a mythic hero, king of the jungle, that kind of stuff. Had a chimp he named Cheetah, and a son he called Boy. I always thought, you know, it was kind of funny how he had a name for his chimp, but not for his kid."

Igneous looked at Hunter blankly. "You know, I've had riders up on insubordination charges for wasting less of my time than you are right now," Igneous said.

"Yeah, okay. Some things just take time to explain," Hunter said. "Especially since we can't use mind talk."

"Get on with it, then!"

"A couple of summers ago, I went to this place named Camp Running Water—but we used to call it Swamp Running Water, because it was all muck and moss and vines and stuff—just like this place."

Igneous shook his head. "It sounds delightful. Are you going to be getting near a point any time soon?"

"Anyway, we used to play Tarzan at camp a lot, running through the forest and swinging on the vines," Hunter said. "I got pretty good at it. I could sneak in, climb a tree, swing down, and grab the shard before any of them even blinks."

"Dragonfly warriors don't blink," Igneous said.

"Before they know what's happening," Hunter explained.

Igneous nodded slowly, appreciatively. "So, Shadow, Flame, and I would wait and rush in to cover your escape if you get into trouble," he said.

"Oh, I'll get into plenty of trouble," Hunter said. "Count on it. But maybe I can get out again before any of it gets me. And if not…" He shrugged. "Then I'll just pull my sword and fight my way out, which was your plan anyway."

Igneous nodded again. "Sometimes, I almost understand why the Oracle chose you to fulfill the prophecy."

"Chose me?" Hunter asked, puzzled. "What do you mean, 'chose me'?"

Igneous didn't answer. "We need to get closer for your plan to work," he said. "We'll ride downhill as far as we can without being seen and then go on foot."

"Sounds good," Hunter replied. "Just be ready to help out when I make my move."

"I'm not sure what that means," Igneous said, "but I'll be ready when the fighting starts."

Hunter grinned at the stern Spider Rider leader and said, "That's what it means."

Dungobeet picked his way up the windswept cliff face, terrified that at any moment he might lose his grip and fall. It was a long way to the bottom of the mountain valley, and the tiny, vestigial wings under Dungo's shell would freeze almost instantly if he tried to fly in this frigid air. So he walked, trudging through the snow up the mountain to meet another of his master's deadly allies.

126

Several of Dungo's messenger bugs circled nearby, but their wings were icing up, and they were neither large enough nor strong enough to help him if he got into trouble. Then again, the dung beetle also feared that if he ever died of thirst in the desert or fell freezing in the snow, his own messenger bugs would devour him. That's how it was with Dungobeet, constant fearing that something, or someone, in this hostile land was going to eat him, and his position as Mantid's messenger made exposure to danger a constant problem.

"Not much farther," he muttered to himself, not quite believing it.

He crested a small rise and paused to rest a moment. The breath wheezed in and out of his spiracles. His messengers buzzed around him insistently.

"I know, I know," he said, more to himself than them, "Mantid is counting on me, and I will die just as surely if I *don't* complete the mission as I would from falling."

But falling wasn't the only way to die on this mission. Dungobeet knew that very well. Danger lurked around every boulder of the Great Mountains. Most dangerous of all was the person Dungo was visiting—the person Mantid had special plans for.

One of the messenger bugs bounced off Dungo's shoulder, as if urging him on.

"I know, I know!" he replied.

He got up and began climbing once more. The Great Mountains loomed over him, their huge bulk sometimes obscuring the molten sun of the Inner World.

Dungobeet knew it would be dark at his destination, and he didn't like the dark.

He crested another rise, and a huge cave opened up before him. The entrance looked like the yawning maw of a giant spider. Its appearance sent a shudder down Dungo's exoskeleton.

"Couldn't she have picked a n-nicer place to live?" he whined to himself.

He pulled his armored body up onto the ledge in front of the cave and peered inside. It was dark. Very dark. He sent two messenger bugs inside. They disappeared into the jet-blackness.

Then he lost contact with them.

Dungobeet swallowed hard. "Perhaps I'm not welcome," he said to himself. He turned as if to go, then froze, caught between his fear of the cave and his fear of Mantid.

"Of course you're not welcome," a high, cold voice said.

Dungo almost jumped out of his shell. He whirled around to see who was about to kill him. When he spotted her, his knees gave way and he collapsed onto the barren rock.

She rode out of the cave astride a giant spider. The arachnid was like none Dungobeet had ever seen. It was shiny, metallic; it hissed and whirred as it moved. Its metal legs clacked and clanked as they strode across the stone of the cave entryway. The creature smelled of oil and lightning. Dungobeet realized suddenly that this was no living creature—it was a machine.

The warrior perched on the spider machine's back was a human female—a teenage girl, as near as Dungobeet could tell (though all humans looked alike to him). She wore armor like a Spider Rider, but her cruel face and cold eyes were different from any Dungo had seen before. She ran her armored hands over a series of spines on the metal creature's back, and it lurched toward him. Its mechanical maw swung open, looking as deadly as the mandibles of any real spider.

Dungo's remaining spy bugs fainted and fell to the ground. The metal spider rose up on its back legs. Before Dungobeet could react, it seized him in its talons.

The cruel-looking girl laughed. "You've come a long way to die, little bug," she said.

Dungobeet could barely find the voice to speak. "G-g-greetings from Mantid the M-m-magnificent," Dungo stuttered. "P-please don't eat me, great Aqune. I bear a m-message from my master!"

The girl, Aqune, looked vaguely amused. "What does the ruler of the Insectors want with me?" she asked. "If this is some kind of trap, I promise you won't live to regret it."

"N-no trap, mistress," Dungo said. "I promise."

She scoffed. "As if Insector promises are worth anything!"

"Worth, perhaps, as much as S-spider Rider promises...?" Dungobeet ventured.

The girl's eyes narrowed. Her armored fists clenched the metal spines on her machine's back. "Why have you come?" she asked.

"G-great Mantid believes that you have been...ill-used by the Spider Riders," Dungobeet said. "Wrongly convicted of treason for your opposition to the Arachna royal family, and banished without just cause. My master therefore thinks that perhaps you and he share a common interest."

"What interest does the lord of the Insectors share with an exiled Spider Rider?" Aqune asked, her lips pulling into a wicked sneer.

"The annihilation of the Spider Riders," Dungobeet said.

Slowly, Aqune smiled. When she spoke again, her voice was almost a purr.

"Tell me more, bug."

17
A Line and a Prayer

Hunter Steele crept through the cypress trees, trying hard not to be seen. He'd changed into pedestrian mode, fearing that his armor might both slow him down and make noise that would give him away.

The problem, of course, was that without his armor, he had little protection if the Insectors did discover him. Though he'd left Igneous, Flame, and Shadow hiding near the base of the mountain only a few minutes earlier, he already felt very much alone.

His mind kept subconsciously asking Shadow for advice and coming up blank. He felt as if part of him had gone missing.

Hunter found a suitable climbing tree. He had been good at tree climbing in the surface world, and these big swamp trees, with their gnarls and twists, were even easier to scale. He quickly made his way to the canopy branches high above. He moved through the treetops carefully but swiftly. In very little time, he reached the edge of the trees circling the clearing.

Hunter peered down at the vast formation of Insectors below. Thankfully, they hadn't yet spotted him.

Hunter touched a few key studs on his manacle. Since he was unarmored, his distance viewer apparatus extended from the bracelet and then crawled, spiderlike, up his arm to his face. He adjusted the focus and range finder, carefully calculating the distance between him and the stolen shard.

It would be a very long, very tricky swing.

Sturdy vines ran through the canopy like great loops of garden hose. Hunter used his viewer to select one the right length to extend across the dragonfly warrior formation. Too short and he would soar past the shard without being able to reach it; too long and he would crash into the formation of Insector warriors.

Despite feeling confident in his plan, Hunter began to sweat.

He retracted his viewer and activated his manacle's energy knife. He took the vine he'd chosen and then turned his back to the dragonflies—to shield the light of the cutter from their multifaceted eyes.

Hands trembling, he cut the vine to the proper length. Then he put away the knife and got a good grip. He twined the vine carefully around his waist, so he'd have one hand free to grab the shard. This was the easy part; escaping after recovering the shard—that would be hard.

Hunter stood on the edge of a big limb, looking down on the warrior formation, and took a deep breath. Sweat beaded on his forehead and dripped into his eyes.

"C'mon," he told himself silently. "You can do this. It's just like summer camp. You've done it a thousand times before."

But here the drop was much longer, and there was no pleasant pond to splash into if the vine snapped. And the shard seemed very, very far away.

Hunter took a deep breath and jumped.

*

Igneous fiddled with the settings on his distance viewer and scanned the warriors' square from his hiding place near the base of the mountain. The trees and dragonfly warriors obscured his view somewhat, but he could still see the shard glittering in the shadows.

"What is that Earthen kid waiting for?" he asked, more to himself than to the spiders waiting with him.

He ran the viewer over the warriors' square, then the canopy above, where he knew Hunter must be hiding. Even knowing what he was up to, Igneous still couldn't spot him. The captain-general nodded appreciatively. Maybe the Earthen did have some skill after all.

Shadow and Flame looked to Igneous for some clue as to what was going on. With mind talk shut down, Igneous could use only hand signals to give them a vague idea of what was about to happen.

Flame seemed content to wait and watch. On the other hand, Shadow's forelimbs twitched impatiently.

Igneous nodded to him. "I know," he said. "It's tough to be without your mind-linked partner. I feel it, too, even though Flame is right here beside me."

Shadow nodded back, though without mind talk, Igneous knew the spider understood little or nothing of what he had just said.

"Don't worry," Igneous continued. "If the Earthen's plan works, you'll be reunited soon enough." He forced a smile. "And if it doesn't work," he thought to himself, "we'll all be reunited…in death."

At that moment, movement from near the warriors' square caught Igneous's attention.

"Great Oracle!" he gasped.

Though they did not understand his words, the spiders snapped to attention.

As the three of them watched, Hunter leaped out of the trees. He swung in a long arc, aiming directly at the tree stump holding the shard.

Igneous gasped again. "He's going to land right in the middle of them!"

Hunter focused on the shard atop the tree stump. He tried not to think about the deadly army surrounding it. He swooped out of concealment, heading directly for his objective. Before the Insectors saw him, he was almost there.

He'd miscalculated, though, and cut his vine a few feet too short.

"I can't reach it!" he thought desperately.

There was only one thing to do. As he swung in, he loosened the vine he'd harnessed around himself. He let the loop slip from his waist down around his legs, and finally to his boots.

The vine might have slipped off entirely, but he cried, "Arachna might!" and activated his Spider Rider armor. Instantly, the armor surrounded his body, making him just a bit larger—enough that the vine noose snagged around his ankles rather than slip away.

Hunter's sudden appearance startled the Insectors. Before they could react, he was past their ranks and over the shard.

He reached out and grabbed. His fingers played over the shard's surface, knocking it from its resting place. The shard slipped out of Hunter's right hand and spun across the top of the tree stump. It toppled toward the edge.

Hunter grabbed it with his left hand just before it went over.

The Insectors shrieked as Hunter soared over their heads. They turned, but not quickly enough, as he swooped past them and arced back up into the air.

Hunter clutched the shard tightly in his left fist and drew his sword with his other hand.

As he reached the apex of his swing, he cut the vine holding his ankles. The vine went slack and fell away.

Hunter flew through the air toward the surrounding cypress trees. He turned his body just enough to avoid crashing into one of the massive trunks.

The marshy ground rushed up fast. He didn't want the shard to hit first, so he twisted in the air to land on his back, clutching the shard tight against his chest.

He hit hard amid a stand of giant ferns. Lights exploded before his eyes, and all the air rushed out of his lungs. He staggered to his feet, unsure for a moment where he was.

Then he heard the buzz of the dragonfly warriors coming after him.

Fungus Brain hissed with surprise and anger. Hot spittle flew from his gaping maw, spraying the dragonfly warriors standing guard nearby. The guards didn't seem to notice, even as the spit began dissolving their chitinous skin.

"What is this?" Fungus Brain hissed, though all those in the chamber with him were mind controlled and therefore unable to reply.

Every second Fungus Brain mentally sifted the input from the subservient brains of thousands of his thralls all over Quagmiro. Usually, when things were going as he expected, that task proved easy. When surprising things happened, though, it sometimes took him a while to adjust. Now was turning out to be one of those times.

His vast intelligence darted around his kingdom, like an angry horsefly flitting among the heads of his many servants. Someone or something had swooped out of the sky and snatched the shard.

"How is this possible?" he raged. "There are no Spider Riders anywhere near the shard! We know exactly where they are! We've heard the puny minds of their spiders! They're moving up the coast to attack the shard from the rear. We've already sent a dragonfly legion to intercept and destroy them!"

He focused his mind on that legion of warriors, now chasing up the coast a good distance away. Fungus Brain's flabby innards ran cold—none of those flying warriors saw the expected contingent of Spider Riders.

Fungus Brain howled a hideous, burbling scream. More acid spittle sprayed onto his enthralled minions.

"False signals!" he shrieked. "False signals! We are tricked!"

In a frenzy of anger he lashed out with his tendrils, snatching up several of his dragonfly guards. He snapped them like twigs and shoveled the still-twitching pieces into his gaping maw.

"Destroy! Destroy the Spider Riders!" he screamed.

All over Quagmiro, his servants snapped to attention and waited for Fungus Brain to show them their target.

But his thoughts were still unfocused and confused as Hunter landed in the bed of ferns beyond the warriors' square.

The dragonfly sentries milled around, uncertain, knowing only that their master's hate filled them with the desire to kill.

Fungus Brain fought down his anger and concentrated, turning all his will to destroying the enemy who had stolen his shard.

"Kill him!" the monstrous brain gurgled. "Kill him and every spider and rider in Quagmiro! Bring us their carcasses so that we may slowly digest their flesh!"

"I am so doomed!" Hunter thought as he ran. "What was I thinking, that they wouldn't notice me as I swung over and grabbed the shard? That I would be able to outrun a couple of thousand winged warriors? Man! If only I'd been able to talk to Shadow, maybe we would have come up with a better plan!"

Hunter tucked the shard into a safe compartment in his armor and kept running. But he wasn't even entirely sure that he was heading in the right direction.

He glanced back and saw a dragonfly warrior coming in fast. Hunter spun with his sword just in time to parry the Insector's hooked spear.

The bug tried to rip the sword out of Hunter's hand, but he held tight. Hunter swung his other fist around and smashed it right into the dragonfly's big eyes. The Insector reeled, and Hunter stunned it with his sword.

By that time, though, more of the swarm had caught up with him.

Hunter kept going, running when he could, turning and fighting when he had to. He felled two more dragonflies, but the next one breathed fire at him.

Hunter was so surprised that he barely remembered to duck.

"Sonic charge!" he cried, focusing some of his scant remaining power into the manacle weapon.

The forest shook with the sound, and several dragonflies fell out of the air. Hunter ran again.

Unfortunately, the trees were thinning out ahead of him. He'd be more vulnerable to the dragonfly attacks in the open, but he didn't have any choice. He had to go into the open and back up the mountain to get out of Quagmiro.

And where was Igneous?

Hunter thought as hard as he could, trying to call his friends with mind talk, even though he knew it had been shut down.

As he concentrated, something hit him hard in the back. Several somethings—dragonfly spears.

The impact of the weapons knocked Hunter face first to the mossy ground.

He turned and saw a huge swarm of dragonfly warriors flying through the air toward him. With no trees for cover and no friends to help him, Hunter knew this was the end.

18
Escape from Quagmiro

Hunter scrambled to his feet and turned to face the enemy. His heart pounded as more than a hundred dragonfly warriors flew toward him.

"Well," Hunter thought, "if they're going to kill me, I'm going to make them pay!"

He readied his stun sword, trying to figure out the best plan of defense. "I'll channel my remaining manacle energy into my shield," he thought. "If I take out this first bunch, maybe I can make it up the mountainside and find the others before I'm fried."

The plan didn't make him feel much less doomed, but at least it gave him a goal to concentrate on.

The dragonfly warriors swooped in, five abreast in their first wave, with three more waves immediately behind.

Hunter gritted his teeth and prepared to die like a Spider Rider.

"Too bad I couldn't have gotten this shard back to Arachnia," he thought. "Maybe it would have been enough to save Petra."

The warriors came at him, swords flashing, eyes filled with hatred.

Then, suddenly, the first wave lost control of their limbs. They hung twitching in the air for a moment, then fell to the ground, stunned, and lay there.

"Shadow!" Hunter blurted as the spider leaped from concealment behind a copse of overgrown bushes just up the mountain slope.

Igneous and Flame bounded after the big black arachnid. Both spiders fired their sleep darts and spun wide capture webs. The darts felled another dozen dragonflies, and the webs tangled up three times as many more.

Shadow extended a foreleg, and Hunter scrambled up onto his back.

"About time you got here!" Hunter said to Igneous.

"You weren't in any danger," Igneous replied. "I'd say we've timed our entrance perfectly." He flashed Hunter a wry smile.

The sudden appearance of the spiders seemed to confuse the dragonflies. They crashed into one another and got even more twisted in the capture webs. Those not entangled looked confused—as though waiting for orders on how to handle the new situation.

Flame and Shadow turned and galloped up the mountainside as quickly as they could.

As they went, Hunter said to Shadow, "What kept you?"

"We had a few things to set up," Shadow replied.

His friend's voice echoing in his head after so long shocked Hunter. "I thought mind talk was shut down," he thought back.

"That was when we were trying to hide from the enemy," Shadow replied. "Now they know where we are." Hunter could almost hear the smile in the spider's voice.

"Well, it's good to have you back," he said. "I missed you."

"And I, you," Shadow replied.

They hurried over the mountain crest and quickly down the other side, toward the tangled swampland below.

Hunter glanced back but saw no sign of the enemy. "Why aren't they following faster?" he asked Igneous.

"I can't be sure," the Spider Rider leader replied, "but I believe that they're being controlled telepathically."

"By the same telepath the spiders sensed earlier?" Hunter asked.

"I think so," Igneous said. "When something unexpected happens, like you grabbing the shard or us ambushing the swarm, it takes their leader a while to adjust and regain control of the Insectors' minds."

"So there are downsides to telepathy," Hunter mused.

"There are always downsides to not thinking for yourself," Igneous noted.

They reached the swampy forest at the mountain's base just as the first dragonfly warriors soared over the mountaintop. Rather than slogging through the mire this time, though, the spiders leaped up to the trees and raced across the top of the canopy.

Hunter's stomach flew into his throat as they dashed over the treetops at a dizzying pace. No human would ever have been able to move so fast, but the battle spiders handled it with ease, distributing their great weight adroitly on the tips of their eight massive legs. They actually distanced themselves a bit from the swarm.

"Why didn't we do this when we first arrived, rather than slogging through the swamp?" Hunter wondered.

"We were trying to be stealthy," Shadow reminded him. "And Brutus was wounded, remember?"

Hunter felt a bit foolish. "Where are Corona and Magma? Are they all right?"

"I sent them on ahead when we reestablished mind link," Igneous explained. "Magma and Brutus are all patched up, and Venus is back from her decoy mind talk mission."

Hunter glanced back over his shoulder. The swarm of dragonflies looked like an immense black cloud in the sky.

"Here they come!" Hunter warned.

Flame and Shadow leaped from the treetops and splashed heavily into the blue-green ocean. Scattered bodies of the defeated Water Strykers still dotted the sea. In the distance, Hunter could dimly see the main continent of Arachnia, looming out of the mist on the horizon.

The battle spiders paddled their legs with all their might. Hunter felt glad that Shadow seemed to have completely gotten over his fear of the ocean.

"No time for fear," Shadow thought back. "We have to get to the mainland before those Insectors roast us."

"Good idea," Hunter agreed. He knew the chances of getting there before the bugs caught them remained slim, though. The dragonflies, now that they had reorganized themselves, flew much faster than the spiders could swim.

"Keep going as long as you can," Igneous ordered. "Try to use what manacle energy you have left for shields alone."

Hunter nodded and glanced down at his manacle. The light was flashing very weakly—he didn't have much power remaining. One good sonic charge would exhaust it completely. He noticed that Igneous's manacle was flashing the same way. If the lead Spider Rider felt any fear, though, he didn't show it.

Hunter looked back—the dragonflies were flying nearer each second. Within moments, they'd be within firing range.

"In this case," Hunter thought, "that means *real* fire!"

"I'm swimming as fast as I can!" Shadow thought, picking up on Hunter's unconscious suggestion.

They plowed through the water, tossing floating bodies of defeated Water Strykers in their wake.

"Shields up!" Igneous ordered.

He and Hunter spun to face the enemy.

The dragonfly warriors swooped in, breathing fire and throwing spears.

The weapons Hunter and Igneous batted aside with their swords; the fire they deflected with their shields. Each bolt they stopped cost them manacle energy.

A few spears got past their defense but bounced harmlessly off Shadow's and Flame's armor. Some fire bolts got through as well. One struck Shadow's flank.

"Sorry!" Hunter said, feeling the big spider's pain through their mind link.

"It's okay," Shadow replied. "Just be sure you get the next one."

Hunter tried, but neither he nor Igneous could stop all the fireballs. Hunter winced every time one of the burning missiles hit Shadow's armored shell.

They darted into a flotilla of web-entangled Strykers, three-quarters of the way to the mainland. The Insector bodies provided some cover from the dragonfly fire but not nearly enough.

Igneous called, "I'm out!"

Hunter glanced down at the crystal in his manacle. "Me, too!" he said.

"Our sleep darts haven't had time to regenerate," Shadow warned.

"Make ready," Igneous commanded. "They're coming in fast and hard."

Hunter nodded, and both riders and spiders turned to face their foes. The Stryker bodies around them would give them some cover, though probably not enough to prevent them from being killed.

The dragonfly warriors swarmed in, sensing the Spider Riders' weakness. They shot fire at their foes, but the bursts fell short.

"Wait for it!" Igneous said.

Hunter was puzzled. "Wait for what?" he thought. "Sudden burning death?"

Just then, a nearby tangle of defeated Strykers heaved up in the sea. A volley of sleep darts raked into the front ranks of the advancing dragonfly warriors.

The stunned Insectors fell into the sea, and those behind them paused in confusion.

Instantly, Venus and Brutus sprang from concealment; they'd camouflaged themselves amid the bodies of the defeated Strykers. Now they quickly climbed atop the floating hulks and cast a pair of huge capture webs. The spiders' great affinity for balance and weight distribution allowed them to stand upon the bobbing corpses.

The webs snared the dragonfly warriors' front ranks. The ranks behind the entangled Insectors crashed into them, making an even bigger mess. All of them spiraled into the ocean with a huge splash.

Venus and the other battle spiders quickly stun-darted the few Insectors remaining in the first wave. The pile of bodies floating atop the water grew.

"Great going!" Hunter shouted, pumping his fist in the air. He barely even minded that Igneous hadn't told him about the trap.

"Igneous is probably worried about mind talk leaking to their telepathic leader," Shadow suggested.

"Yeah, right," Hunter muttered, unconvinced.

"The ambush has bought us only a little time," Igneous said, both speaking and using mind talk. "Swim for shore as fast as you can!"

Even though the first wave of dragonfly warriors was floundering in the ocean, a second, larger wave was flying close behind.

All four spiders swam toward shore as quickly as they could. Their legs kicked up huge fountains of spray as they went.

Hunter glanced back at the Insectors. Igneous was right— they'd bought themselves only a little time. He caught Corona's eye and gave her a thumbs-up. She smiled and returned the gesture.

"You got here just in time," he said, trying to use the mind link between Shadow and Venus to talk to Corona.

"Igneous is a great tactician," she replied. "He sent the four of us ahead to set the trap even as you and he escaped with the shard."

Hunter felt glad that he was getting better at mind talk, but he was annoyed that Igneous had outthought *him*—as well as the Insectors—in this instance.

"How's Magma?" he asked. He couldn't see the big Turandot through the spray the spiders were kicking up.

"Better, but not at full strength yet," Corona replied.

"Don't worry about Magma, Hunter," Venus interjected. "His experience will see him through. Just take care of yourself."

"You bet," Hunter told the spider. In a hidden part of his mind, he boiled at the implication that he might *not* be able to take care of himself.

The buzzing noise behind them grew louder. Hunter glanced back and saw the dragonfly warriors closing in once more. The mainland forests lay dead ahead, but the riders wouldn't get there before the next swarm caught up.

"Keep going as long as you can!" Igneous said. "Corona, protect our rear!"

"Check!" Corona replied.

She and Venus fell back, behind the rest.

Hunter's heart sank. "Go back!" he thought to Shadow. "We have to help her!"

"Flame says no," Shadow replied. "And Venus does, too. Corona still has some manacle power left. She's really good at conserving her energy. She can buy us some time to get to shore."

"But she'll be killed!" Hunter thought desperately.

Corona's voice suddenly intruded into the mind talk link. "Hunter," she said, "you have to learn to trust your fellow riders!"

With that, she turned and threw all of her remaining power into her lightning lance. A huge bolt of blue-white electricity blasted from her armored hands. The Insector swarm scattered, and many of them fell into the sea, stunned or dead.

There were too many, though, and they quickly regrouped.

By then, Corona and Venus had turned for shore again. The other spiders swam ahead of her, but not far enough ahead to make much difference.

A terrible thought flashed through Hunter's mind. "We're not going to make it!"

19
The Last Shard

"Don't think that we're not going to make it!" Shadow replied, but Hunter could feel the worry in the spider's gut, too.

Magma and Brutus had fallen behind the rest. Hunter couldn't tell whether they intended to help Corona and Venus or if their wounds were slowing them down.

"We should help them," Hunter thought again.

"Keep going!" Igneous ordered, as though reading his mind. "We're almost there! If we can make it to land, the dragonflies lose their advantage."

Hunter wasn't so sure. Even if the riders managed to reach the shore, they were still pretty much out of manacle energy. Plus, their spiders were tired and would need time to replenish their sleep darts. The forest might protect them from the flying Insectors, and their webs might buy them some time, but...

The dragonfly warriors dived at Corona and Magma, spraying the Spider Riders with fire. The two riders used what little remained of their manacle energy to activate their shields. Everyone, including the enemy, knew that protection wouldn't last long.

Hunter turned and channeled the last of the life-support energy from his manacle into a final sonic charge. The power screamed from his manacle and blasted the dragonflies near his friends. But the weapon was so weak that it made the Insectors pause for only half a moment.

Hunter expected Igneous to rebuke him, but just then, the rider leader used all his remaining manacle energy in a final stun blast.

The detonation did little more damage than Hunter's charge did, though their combined efforts bought Corona, Magma, and their spiders a few more seconds of life.

"Go!" Corona screamed at Hunter. Venus and Brutus swam as quickly as they could, but already the volley of drag-onfly fire was taking its toll on the battle spiders.

Hunter's heart felt torn in two. He needed to get the shard back to Arachnia to help Petra and all the Turandot people, but he couldn't bear to leave Corona and Magma and their noble spiders to die.

Apparently, Shadow couldn't bear the idea, either. In sync with Hunter's thought, he turned to make one final, desper-ate stand. Hunter drew his lance. Though he had no experi-ence jousting on the water, he hoped the long spear might enable him to hit the dragonflies before they hit him.

Igneous shouted something, but the blood was pounding in Hunter's ears. Had Igneous said, "No!" or was it…?

"Now!" Igneous cried again.

As the dragonfly warriors swooped in for the kill, a barrage of sleep darts shot from the forest on the mainland shore. The darts struck the startled front rank of dragonfly warriors, knocking them from the sky.

Immediately, manacle blasts of all kinds blazed from the trees, mowing down the Insectors behind the first swarm.

The startled bugs paused, uncertain what to do.

"Again!" came a cry from shore. Hunter recognized the voice as Prince Lumen's. In the same instant, he and Shadow realized what was happening.

"Lumen's brought the legions to cover our escape!" Shadow thought. His joy at the realization spilled over the mind link into Hunter's mind.

As the first wave of dragonfly warriors flopped into the sea, a whole regiment of Spider Riders emerged from the woods on shore, Prince Lumen at their lead.

They fired stun blasts, lightning, fire, sonic charges, and a dozen other manacle weapons at the surprised Insectors. A legion of spiders strafed the dragonfly swarm with sleep darts.

Hunter and the others cheered and then swam quickly to shore under covering fire from their friends. By the time Igneous, Hunter, and Corona helped Magma and Brutus out of the water, Lumen's contingent had swept the skies almost clean of dragonflies. Many lay unmoving in the water, and more were trapped in sticky capture webs. Only a few managed to flit on wounded wings back to Quagmiro.

Prince Lumen grinned from ear to ear. "A fine plan, Igneous," he said.

"And executed to perfection, my prince," Igneous replied.

"I did okay, too! Didn't I!" said an excited voice. All the riders turned to see Princess Sparkle emerge from the crowd.

Lumen frowned. "Sparkle," he said, "how did you get here? I ordered you to remain in the castle!"

She crinkled her nose at him. "How will Hotarla and I ever learn anything if you're always leaving us home?" she asked.

"I expect you to learn *in school*," Lumen replied, "in the Children's Brigades like every other rider in training."

She scoffed. "That's not how Hunter learned!" she said. "Besides, every other Spider Rider isn't a princess!"

"You'll never be a Spider Rider if you keep this up," Lumen said angrily.

"And I'd pick another role model, if I were you," Igneous warned. "The Earthen still has a lot to learn."

Hunter fumed silently. "Just when I thought we were doing all right," he mind-talked to Shadow, "Igneous has to rain on my parade!"

"We're having a parade?" Shadow said. "Great!"

After they returned to the city, Igneous, Corona, Magma, and Hunter assembled in the castle's throne room.

Prince Lumen paced the stone floor as King Arachna listened patiently from his throne. Seated on a smaller throne near his left elbow, Princess Sparkle fidgeted. They'd tried to exclude her from the meeting, but she would have none of it. Lumen couldn't figure out a way to get rid of her without making a scene.

"After all," her father concluded, "she, too, will rule one day, Lumen. How can she gain experience if you are always shooing her out of the room?"

Lumen didn't have a good reply to that, so he just scowled and paced some more.

"This new threat from Quagmiro is troublesome," the prince said. "I wish we knew more about the power controlling the dragonfly warriors. We'll have to fortify the city defenses to counter an airborne assault, just as we did during the locust wars."

"Surely, Quagmiro's power is spent for the moment, my son," the king said. "They have suffered a devastating defeat at the hands of your riders. They'll not trouble us for some time, I expect."

"You never know what to expect from Insectors!" Lumen snapped.

"I'll see that the airborne defenses are fortified," Igneous said.

"Perhaps the Oracle could shed some light on what kind of attack we might expect next," King Arachna suggested.

The prince slapped his head. "Of course! I'm so worried about the war, I've forgotten the next step in the battle."

The prince opened the secret entrance to the passage leading to the Oracle chamber. He and the other Spider Riders went inside. The king remained in the throne room to tend to the other affairs of the kingdom.

"Stay with me, Sparkle," he said.

The princess nodded as if she would. Then, just before the secret entrance slid closed, she ducked inside.

"Sorry, Daddy!" she called back. Then, to her brother and the others, she shouted, "Wait for me!"

Mantid stood in the communication chamber and stared at the small piece of Fungus Brain that connected him to Quagmiro's tyrant.

"What?" the Insector ruler asked, not believing what he had just heard.

"The Spider Riders escaped our trap!" Fungus Brain fumed.

"You failed," Mantid said.

Fungus Brain burbled and hissed with hatred at the suggestion. "There were circumstances you did not inform us about," he said.

"Such as?" Mantid asked.

"They employed tactics other than those your spies had reported to us," Fungus Brain said.

"You're supposed to be the telepath," Mantid said. "Did you not…foresee them?"

The image of Fungus Brain grew livid with anger. His tentacles flailed wildly in the air. "They interfered with our telepathy," he said, "sent out false messages…"

"As *you* were supposed to do, so they would not discover the shard," Mantid said, his voice low and lethal.

"Two thousand guards surrounded that shard!" Fungus Brain said.

"Clearly not enough to defeat one small contingent of Spider Riders," Mantid said.

"Your forces have fared no better!" the Brain countered.

"True," Mantid said. "That is why I have set other plans in motion."

"What about our alliance?" Fungus Brain asked. "You promised to make us one of the Big Four!"

"Consider the offer and the alliance…terminated," Mantid said.

He brought one scythelike claw down on the pulsing thing atop the pedestal. The claw smashed the brain matter into jelly and reduced the pedestal to shards. The image of Fungus Brain vanished.

Mantid licked the claw clean and left the room.

Lumen placed the seventh shard in the Oracle's crown. The glow around her increased, and her features grew more distinct. Another arm unfolded itself from her chest. The arm's fist opened, and in it a bright new flame sprang to life.

Lumen and the other Spider Riders smiled.

The Oracle's gentle, musical voice filled each of their minds. "Again, you have done well, my heroic Spider Riders," she said. "You have my eternal gratitude."

Hunter stepped forward. "What about Petra?" he asked. "Can you cure her now?"

"I am nearly whole," the Oracle said, "but my power is not complete. I cannot both protect the city of Arachnia and rescue the lost rider from death's doorstep."

Hunter was crestfallen. "I'd hoped…" he began.

Corona put her hand on his shoulder. "We *all* hoped," she said.

"Hope isn't enough, though," Igneous said. "We must keep working, battle the enemy, find the final shard, and return it to where it belongs."

"I'll be right there with you!" Sparkle put in.

Lumen glared at her. "This battle is not for you, Sparkle," he said. "You have not yet taken the tests. You are not yet a Spider Rider. This is *our* fight, not yours."

Igneous, Magma, and Corona nodded their agreement.

"We've trained for this," Corona said. "We'll find the shard or die trying."

"Those trained will not find it," the Oracle said. "It is not their fate."

All of them turned to face her, stunned. "What…?" the three older riders asked simultaneously.

"You mean we're *all* going to die trying?" Magma said. He didn't seem afraid, just disappointed.

"No, brave Magma," the Oracle replied. "Only *one* will find the shard. The rest are appointed other missions."

154

"But the final shard must be the best guarded of all," Lumen said. "It will take every Spider Rider I have to rescue it."

"Every Spider Rider would fail," the Oracle said.

Everyone in the room was crestfallen.

"But where many would fail," the Oracle continued, "*one* might succeed. Only one will enter Mantid's fortress—one rider alone."

Every person in the room held their breath.

Finally, Hunter asked, "Which one?"

20
The One Chosen

The Oracle gazed benevolently at the boy from the surface world and smiled.

"You, Hunter Steele," she said.

"What!" Lumen blurted.

"Hunter Steele is the chosen one," the Oracle repeated. "He is the one who shall retrieve the last shard and make me whole."

"B-but…" Lumen stuttered, "he's not even royal born! Surely someone of royal blood should undertake such an important task."

"My brother's right," Sparkle said, stepping up beside Lumen. "What's the point of being a princess—or a prince— if other people get to do all the important stuff?"

Lumen glared at his sister, but Hunter thought he shared her feelings.

"We all have our roles to play, my young rider-to-be," the Oracle said calmly. "Everything in the Inner World has its place. It is Hunter's place to go on this mission."

Hunter swallowed hard. He felt both honored and, at the same time, scared. "So, I'm supposed to go to Mantid's fortress alone?"

"Only your spider may accompany you," the Oracle said.

Magma crossed his arms over his massive chest. "The boy's talented," he said, "but too young."

"And too inexperienced as well," Igneous interjected. "Let me—or one of the other riders—go with him."

"Let all of us go," Corona suggested. "We work well as a team. The journey will be safer, too."

Hunter felt torn. He was glad that Corona felt concerned for him. At the same time, he was a bit annoyed that no one seemed to think he could handle this on his own.

Slowly, the statue of the Oracle shook her head. "No," she said. "The rest of you are needed elsewhere. This task is for Hunter and Shadow alone. It is for this task that he was chosen." She looked at the boy from Earth, her eyes full of confidence.

Hunter took a deep breath and nodded. "Of course I'll do it," he said.

The Oracle cast her gaze over the others in the chamber. One by one, they all nodded their assent, though Sparkle seemed reluctant to do so.

"Your will be done, great Oracle," Lumen said through clenched teeth.

"Mantid will be expecting an attack," the Oracle said, "so we will send a great force of Spider Riders along the shores of Lake Arachnia toward the main entrance to his castle."

Lumen and Igneous nodded.

"A decoy," Magma said appreciatively.

"Yes," the Oracle replied. "Hunter Steele will launch the true assault. He will go through the mountains to the far side of Mantid's fortress. My telepathic probes show the rear of the castle is sparsely guarded. Hunter and Shadow will find a way in, and Hunter shall take it. Shadow will come to the Earthen's aid if it becomes necessary."

Hunter nodded. "I guess a battle spider in the castle would attract more attention than one lone rider."

"But that's practically suicide!" Sparkle blurted. "I take back what I said earlier! I don't care if Hunter's not noble born, I don't want him to get killed!"

"Fear not, child," the Oracle said. "It is not Hunter's fate to be killed inside Mantid's castle."

Sparkle didn't seem very reassured, but Hunter said, "Don't worry. Shadow and I can take care of ourselves."

Sparkled nodded, though her eyes looked somewhat misty.

"It is vital," the Oracle said, "that no one outside this room should know of Hunter's true mission. Mantid's spies—both physical and telepathic—are everywhere."

"We understand," Igneous said. "Every member of our diversion force shall believe that we're actually planning to attack Mantid."

"Go now," the Oracle said, her aura fading. "Prepare yourselves."

Swirling black clouds brooded over the fortress of Mantid the Magnificent. Lightning flashes illumined the forbidding castle, as well as the jagged mountain peaks nearby.

As cold rain pelted the stone walls of the stronghold, Dungobeet opened the doorway to Mantid's audience chamber. Inside, Buguese, Royal Beerain, and Grasshop sat in their places, behind the room's meeting table. In the shadows, on a raised dais at the room's center, sat Mantid. His armor glistened in the reflected light from the storm outside, and his malevolent eyes gleamed red.

Dungobeet scurried to one side of the doorway, anxious to get out of the way of their visitor. Several of his messenger bugs darted after him and buzzed around nervously.

The beetlelike Insector bowed low. "Master," Dungo said, "I have done as you requested. I have brought you Aqune the renegade, mistress of the metal spiders."

With a whir and a clank and a scraping of metal claws, Aqune's great spider-shaped machine appeared in the doorway. She released the spines behind its head and stepped down onto the audience chamber's polished marble floor.

Her cold, calculating eyes glanced around the room, taking in both the surroundings and the Insectors seated within. The look on her lean, wolfish face said that she wasn't much impressed.

"So, this is the fortress of Mantid the Magnificent," she said. "No wonder you want to take over Arachnia."

"Before the humans came," Buguese said calmly, "all of the Inner World belonged to the Insectors. Our master merely wishes to return things to their natural state."

Aqune laughed. "Every tyrant insists that his way is the way things were meant to be. If you asked the Spider Riders, they'd say that they were the rightful rulers of this place, too."

"And what do *you* say?" Mantid asked from the shadows. The tone of his deep voice made Aqune pause and look carefully at him. She nodded, impressed.

"I say that the strong take what they want," she replied. "That's the way of the Inner World."

"And your way as well, rider?" Beerain asked.

Aqune's eyes narrowed. "Of course." She turned back to Mantid. "Now, about our business," she began. "Your bug here says that you're interested in wiping out the Spider Riders. Is that true?"

Mantid nodded.

A cruel smile flashed across Aqune's face. "Then I'm your girl."

"I suspected as much," Mantid said. "You will take Stags's place as a member of the Big Four."

Aqune glanced disdainfully at Beerain, Buguese, and Grasshop. "I've never been much of a joiner," she said. "I work better on my own."

"But our purposes coincide," Grasshop said. As he spoke he manipulated another of his inventions, a tiny prismlike machine that cast rays of dancing light around the room. With a twist of a knob, the lights coalesced on the table before him. They formed into a three dimensional image of the Spider Rider city. Another twist of a knob made the city appear to catch fire.

"Nice trick," Aqune said, flashing him a half smile. "It'll take more than tricks, though, to bring down Arachnia."

"That, I believe, is why you are here," Buguese said.

Beerain looked angrily from the human girl to the Insector leader. "You're wasting your time, great Mantid," she said. "This…human and her toy spider can be no match for the Spider Riders."

Aqune looked coldly at her. "But I don't have just one metal spider, bee brat," she said. "I have *many*—as many as Lumen and the rest have battle spiders. And my spiders *never* get tired. They never eat, they never sleep, and wounds cause them no pain. They'll fight until every last Spider Rider is dead." She folded her arms across her chest and smiled.

"Which is why I summoned you," Mantid said. "Now, about *our* plans to destroy the Spider Riders…"

21
The Final Mission

"I don't get it," Geode said to Corona as they rode together amid the huge mass of Spider Riders heading for Mantid's lair. "That Earthen has proved both tough and useful in the past. Why was he selected to stay behind on this mission? We're going to need every rider we've got."

Corona shrugged. "The Oracle's decisions are wise beyond our understanding," she replied.

"I'll tell you why," Crystal put in. She was riding on the other side of Corona, in standard Lost Legion formation. "He got left behind because he wasn't up to the job. He's not one of us—he's just an outsider. Either the Oracle didn't trust his loyalties or she didn't trust his guts."

"That's not true," Corona snapped.

Crystal smiled slightly, and Corona chided herself for letting the girl goad her.

"Stay calm," Venus thought in Corona's mind. "You know she wants to lead the legion, rather than you."

"If Hunter succeeds," Corona thought back, "neither Crystal nor I will be leading the Lost Legion. With her power restored, the Oracle will heal Petra and she can take command again."

"If the Oracle wills it," Venus replied.

The spider's steadying influence helped Corona master her anger. When she replied to Crystal, her voice was calm and commanding. "Hunter Steele has proved his bravery many times," Corona said. "Clearly, the Oracle has need of him elsewhere during this mission."

"True enough," Venus mind-talked to Corona. "Of course, we can't tell Crystal that Hunter is *not* staying behind in the city."

"I wouldn't blame him if he were scared," Geode mused. "I'm a bit nervous myself—and I've been a Spider Rider longer than Hunter has." He smiled and adjusted his stance on the back of his spider, Coal.

Crystal laughed and shook her head. Her silken blond hair whipped through the hot air in a shimmering wave. "Listen to you, Geode!" she said. "It's as if you're a webling just past your tests! These are Insectors! No more, no less. We've fought them and won many times before."

Geode turned slightly red. "Go chew on a web, Crys," he said. "You've been a pain ever since Petra went down."

Crystal's face hardened in an instant.

Before she could respond, though, Corona broke in. "Enough. Do you want Mantid's legions to hear you all the way to his fortress?"

"What's the trouble back here?" asked Igneous. He and Flame had fallen back from the front of the huge column of riders. "Lumen and Ebony seem to think something's going on."

"No trouble, Igneous," Corona said, shooting Geode and Crystal stern looks.

"No trouble," Geode agreed.

"None at all," Crystal added, not quite convincingly.

"Good," the Spider Rider captain said. "The last thing we need is dissent in the ranks during a mission of this importance. All of you remember that." He gazed sternly at each of them, though it was clear he wasn't speaking to Corona.

"Tell the prince not to worry, Igneous," Corona said. "Everything is under control."

"I feel like my whole life is spinning out of control," Hunter confided to Shadow. "I mean, what am I doing here, riding alone into Mantid's fortress? This is nuts!"

Even though Shadow was with him, Hunter had felt lost ever since they'd secretly left Arachnia city. They were moving very quickly in order to reach Mantid's fortress before the other Spider Riders. Lumen's mission, after all, was not to battle the Insectors, but merely to provide distraction for Hunter's commando raid.

If Hunter and Shadow could retrieve the shard before Lumen's regiments got into any actual fighting...Well, then the chances of another Spider Rider ending up like Petra—or worse—would be greatly reduced. Still, at the moment, the burden of it all felt overwhelming to the boy from the surface world.

The landscape became a blur as Hunter and Shadow raced through the forests toward the distant mountains. They'd set their armor to camouflage mode and blended in nicely with the greenery. Insector spies would need to look very carefully to spot them.

"The Oracle wouldn't have chosen you if she didn't know you could complete the mission," Shadow said calmly.

"And about that," Hunter said, "why *did* she choose me? And why did Igneous say that she'd *chosen* me to fulfill the prophecy? He said that even before we'd been assigned this mission."

"The Oracle is very powerful and can see many paths," Shadow said. "It's likely that she foresaw your coming to the Inner World."

Hunter folded his arms over his armored chest. "I'm not sure that I like that," he said.

"Why not?" Shadow asked. "It is an honor to serve destiny."

Hunter frowned. "See, where I come from, we have something called free will. That means that we get to make our own choices in life. We get to control our own destinies."

"That's a foolish idea," Shadow said. "No one gets to make his own choices. Life dictates the choices we make. Do you think I would have chosen you if I had any other choice? No offense."

Despite the spider's gentle tone, Hunter was offended. "That's not the point," he said hotly. "Sure, sometimes we make choices because we have to—like I decided to keep my friend Dave from falling into that gravel pit and ended up here by mistake—but most of the time, we get to do what we want."

"Really?" the spider said, puzzled. "That's not the way we spiders see things. I don't think the Turandot see things that way, either. And I'm sure the Insectors don't."

"Of course they don't!" Hunter said, getting exasperated. "They're just giant bugs, not people!"

Shadow's mind grew dark within Hunter's consciousness. "So, I'm not 'people' either?" the spider said.

"That's not what I mean!" Hunter rolled his eyes and sighed. "That's what I get for trying to talk philosophy with a spider!"

"Some of the greatest philosophers of all time were spiders," Shadow countered.

"I give up!" Hunter said.

"A wise decision," Shadow replied. "Fate—and history—are against you."

After a long, tiring ride, Hunter and Shadow prepared for sleep by fastening a cocoon to a sprawling fern tree in the middle of the forest. Because the sun never set in Arachnia, there was no real way to tell how long they'd been riding. Hunter figured it must have been most of a surface world day.

They'd made good progress—slipping past the far side of the Cavern of Cocoons, while the rest of the Spider Riders marched between the cavern and Lake Arachnia. Hunter was sorry that they hadn't come closer to the Falls from Below. These amazing waterfalls fell skyward, rather than toward the ground. He liked the falls, but this time he'd only glimpsed them from far away. Corona and the rest would see the falls, and the rainbows that often surrounded them, close up.

The volcanic mountains sheltering Mantid's fortress loomed beyond the forest, like a mirage hovering above the treetops. Now Hunter and Shadow were working to camouflage their spider-silk "tent" with leaves, to keep it from being seen while they slumbered.

"I wonder what the others are doing right now," Hunter said as he cut another branch.

"Corona and the rest are probably doing the same thing we are," Shadow replied. "They must be tired as well. Ouch!"

"What's the matter?" Hunter asked, pausing as he fastened another branch to the outside of the cocoon.

"Nothing," the spider replied. "I've just been very stiff since our swim to Quagmiro. Sometimes I feel like I can barely run another mile." He used his huge mandibles to snip off another fern and then affixed the plant to the tent.

"Do you think the water could have gotten into your joints somehow?" Hunter asked. "Is that possible?" He wracked his brains for facts about spiders from his world but could come up with nothing that might compare. On earth, spiders either swam, or they skimmed over the water, or they sank, or they drowned. He'd never heard of one swimming and then suffering for it later.

"How am I supposed to know?" Shadow replied. "I told you I'd never been swimming like that before."

"It's too bad we can't ask Corona or Venus," Hunter said.

"Even if they were within range, we probably shouldn't communicate with them," Shadow said. "Using long-range mind talk might give away where we are and what we're doing."

"You're right," Hunter said. "Will you be able to continue the mission?"

"I believe I should be able to—" Shadow began.

Then something jumped out at them from the forest.

22
The Secret Way

The shape moved with surprising quickness and agility. Hunter and Shadow whirled, but it was already right next to them.

Hunter reached for his sword, then realized who it was. "Sparkle!" he said angrily. "What are you doing here?"

The girl took a deep breath and put on her bravest face. Her spider, Hotarla, puffed up as well, trying to look big and impressive, though she was still a very small spider. "I came to help you," Sparkle said.

"But Lumen ordered you to remain in the city," Hunter replied.

Sparkle stuck out her chest. "I'm a *princess*," she said. "I don't have to answer to my brother. We're both of equal rank."

"Not in the Spider Riders," Hunter said. "And if you ever want to be a Spider Rider, you'd better get back to the city."

Sparkle's lower lip trembled, just slightly. "But I want to help," she pleaded.

"Sparkle, go home," Hunter said politely but firmly.

She crossed her arms over her chest. "No," she said. "You can't order me around. I'm a princess...and I order you to let me help you."

"Shadow," Hunter said aloud, "send a message to Lumen and tell him we've found his sister."

But Sparkle saw through his bluff. "You can't mind-talk that far," she said. "And even if you could, you wouldn't want to telepathically give away your position."

Hunter quietly growled in frustration. "Okay," he said finally. "How do you intend to 'help' me?"

"Watch this," Sparkle said. Her fingers danced over the designs on her manacle, and she squeezed her eyes shut. Much to Hunter's and Shadow's amazement, she slowly faded from view.

"What…?" Hunter sputtered. "How…?"

"I added a new power to my manacle," Sparkle said, her voice seeming to come from thin air. "Hotarla and I can become invisible."

"That's…kind of amazing," Hunter said.

"Isn't it?" she replied. "It was hard to get used to at first, but we've been practicing a lot—whenever we could, really. Now we're good at it."

Hunter had to agree. He couldn't see either the spider or the girl at all. "Does your family know about this?"

Sparkle and Hotarla became visible again. "No," Sparkle replied, frowning. "It's our secret. And don't you tell them!"

Hotarla became visible, too. The spider looked very stern, as if to reinforce her mistress's command.

"So how does this help me?" Hunter asked.

"We can extend our power to you if you link with us," Sparkle said. "That means that you can sneak right up to Mantid's fortress without anyone seeing you."

"But that would mean you'd have to go to the fortress with us," Hunter said.

"That's right," Sparkle agreed.

Hunter thought quickly, trying to come up with some excuse not to take her. Clearly, he couldn't put the princess in such terrible danger.

"But the Oracle said I had to go alone," he countered. "The mission will fail if I don't go alone."

Sparkle frowned and her eyes misted up a bit. Then her face brightened. "Then I'll go with you as far as I can," she said, "but I won't go into the fortress."

"You're not going to win this argument, Hunter," Shadow said to him.

"Okay," Hunter said, feeling exasperated, "you can escort me into the mountains, but once we come within sight of the fortress, you have to turn back. Understand?"

Sparkle and Hotarla both nodded.

Hunter and Shadow helped them build a second camouflaged cocoon tent. Then all four of them slept.

There was no morning when they woke. The Inner World sun blazed just as red as it had when they'd gone to sleep. Hunter, Sparkle, and Hotarla felt refreshed and ready to go. Hunter, though, picked up some pain from Shadow's mind.

"What's wrong?" he asked.

"Just stiff," the spider replied. "Don't worry about it. We should get going."

Hunter and Sparkle mounted up, and the four of them cruised through the forest toward the distant volcanic mountains. They didn't use Sparkle's invisibility power as they went, having decided to save that only for exposed places nearer the fortress.

"A power like that has to use a lot of manacle energy," Shadow said. "We need to make sure she has enough left to get back to the city."

Hunter silently agreed.

The four of them moved as swiftly as only battle spiders could. The huge arachnids' many legs propelled them down the trails as quickly as an SUV might have done on the world above.

All too soon they reached the bleak, desolate lands at the base of the volcanic mountains. In the distance, amid clouds and flashes of lightning, they could just make out the tall, narrow towers of Mantid's fortress.

"Okay," Hunter said to Sparkle, "now's the time."

"Link manacles with me," the princess replied.

Normally, they would have just held hands, but that was impossible while riding their spiders. Hunter concentrated, and a small, spidery carving on the surface of his bracelet came to life. It launched itself through the air and grabbed Sparkle's manacle. A thin, sturdy metal line now connected the two of them.

"Good," Sparkle said, seeming a little bit nervous. She furrowed her brow, and slowly, all four of them faded from view.

"Neat!" Hunter said.

It took him and Shadow a bit of time to get used to moving invisibly. Fortunately, Hotarla could share what she'd learned with Shadow via mind talk.

The learning cost them only a little time, and soon they were moving at top speed through the mountainous terrain.

Hunter found the invisible parts of the journey a bit disconcerting. Since he couldn't see either himself or Shadow, he felt as if he was watching a movie flash by all around him. He had to fight hard to keep from becoming queasy.

As they rode ever higher into the storm-darkened skies, Hunter thought back over his life in the Inner World.

"Not so long ago I was just an ordinary school kid," he told Shadow. "And look where I am now—I'm a hero, trying to save the world."

"Something like that," Shadow said.

"I just hope I don't end up being a *dead* hero," Hunter said.

"Me, too," agreed Shadow as they leaped over a crevasse in the mountainside and landed on the rocky surface beyond.

Hotarla stumbled during her landing, and Hunter felt a telepathic moment of panic from all of his companions. The young spider found her feet again, though, and the four of them continued bravely onward.

As they rode, Hunter wondered where Corona and the others were and what they were doing.

"She's doing her part," Shadow assured him. "Just as we're doing ours."

They slept again in the mountains, this time under the shadow of the thunderclouds. A cloudburst during the night soaked their cocoon tents, but the spiders and humans inside remained dry. The rain had passed by the time they set out again.

Hunter had gotten used to moving invisibly and greatly appreciated the advantage it gave them. They now used the power even more sparingly—only when they were within the fortress's line of sight.

Finally, they rounded a jagged prominence on the mountainside, and the ominous fortress loomed before them.

It was a citadel of spikes and sharp angles. The fortress walls were sheer polished granite and seemed to spring straight up out of the mountainside. Sawtooth crenellations, like the dorsal spines of a giant bug, topped the battlements.

Pointed marble towers dotted with crystal windows thrust into the stormy sky. Red fires burned behind the windows, giving them the appearance of insect eyes gleaming in the darkness. The balconies jutting from the walls of the castle were ragged and asymmetrical. They resembled the broken jawbones of giant insects.

The whole fortress looked like a titanic mutated bug clinging to the mountainside, waiting to pounce on its prey.

Hunter signaled everyone to duck back, and they quickly retreated behind an outcropping of rock.

"Sparkle, this is as far as you go," Hunter said.

"But—" the princess began. She was stubborn, even though Hunter could see the weariness in her every movement. The power crystal on her manacle blinked faintly but steadily.

"Hunter's right," Shadow said on the link, so that the princess and Hotarla could hear him as well. "You've done far more than anyone could have expected or asked. Now you must return home."

Reluctantly, Sparkle and Hotarla nodded. The princess leaped spider-to-spider onto Shadow's back and shook Hunter's hand.

"Good luck," she said.

"You, too," he replied, taken aback.

Impetuously, she kissed him on the cheek. "For luck," she said, blushing.

Hunter nodded but his voice failed him.

Sparkle then leaped back onto Hotarla, and the two of them rode downhill and out of sight.

Hunter took a deep breath. Then he and Shadow stepped out from behind the outcrop of rock and headed for Mantid's fortress.

23
Fortress of Fate

Hunter and Shadow kept close to the rocks, using their camouflage ability as they moved toward Mantid's fortress.

The fortress loomed up on the far side of a deep crevasse, clinging to a high peak. The whole place looked predatory, even the inner castle, where the walls were made of gleaming white marble, crystal, or glass.

"Nice place," Hunter commented, meaning exactly the opposite.

"A nice guy lives there," Shadow replied. The spider was starting to pick up on Hunter's manner of speaking.

Hunter smiled and he felt Shadow smile as well.

They moved cautiously forward, taking advantage of boulders, brush, and other cover to supplement their armor's camouflage. Soon, there was nothing between them and the fortress except the empty air of the yawning chasm.

Hunter activated his armor's distance viewer and took a closer look. On one side, the wall of the castle actually melded with the outer fortifications. The wide gorge itself was the castle's most formidable defense at this point.

Several cockroach guards patrolled the wall of the fortress. Hunter saw other guards through the windows of the castle as they marched down its corridors. Hunter timed the Insectors as they moved across the parapets or past the openings in the huge stone walls.

"The Oracle was right," he said to Shadow. "There aren't many guards on this side."

"That's good," Shadow said, and Hunter felt a twinge of pain across their telepathic link. He looked at Shadow, but the spider didn't say anything.

"We're lucky the castle merges with the outer wall there," Hunter continued. "It's a flaw in their defenses. A Spider Rider army would be cut down before they could climb up, but one Spider Rider might just make it."

"The Oracle was right," Shadow said quietly. "'Where many would fail, *one* might succeed.'"

"The guards are patrolling at regular intervals," Hunter noted. "We have to time our movements so I reach the outer wall between their rounds."

"I'm still feeling a little stiff," Shadow said, "but even if I wasn't, I don't think I could jump that far."

"Can you shoot a web line that far?"

The spider mentally estimated the distance from where they stood to a window in the castle wall on the other side. The window was nearly on the same level they were. "I can," Shadow said, "though the wind will make it a tricky shot. And it will take you a long time to climb across. I doubt you can make it without being seen."

Hunter nodded. "That's what I think, too," he replied via mind talk. "Come on—if we climb higher, I can slide down the rope all the way to the other side."

"That will be pretty dangerous," Shadow said. "I could shoot several webs over and cross them with you on my back."

Hunter shook his head. "We don't have time for that, either, and it's almost sure to get us spotted. I can do this. I've seen it done in the circus and on TV."

"The mysterious teevee again," Shadow said. "You seem to have learned a lot from it."

"Yeah, maybe," Hunter said, "Are you ready?"

Shadow nodded. "I guess..."—he paused and winced—"we'll go with your plan, then."

A look of concern crossed Hunter's face. "Are you *sure* you're all right?" he asked.

"I'll be fine," Shadow said. "Let's get going."

They quickly climbed up the rock face to the next ledge, making sure to stay out of sight of the guards.

They waited until the sentries passed by again, and then Shadow peeked out and shot his web line.

The wind howling through the mountains caught it and pulled it away from his target. Shadow let the line go.

"Good try," Hunter thought.

"I need to adjust for the wind," Shadow replied.

When the guard passed again, Shadow took the wind into account and fired another line. It stuck to the castle wall slightly above one of the windows. The line was very strong but also very fine—it was nearly impossible to see in the storm-clouded darkness.

Lightning flashed and the guard passed by the window once more. He didn't see the line, nor did the guard patrolling the parapet below, who passed by a few moments later.

"Now!" Hunter thought. He had wrapped his armored hands in slick, nonsticky spider silk so they'd slide better. He grasped the line with both hands and threw himself off the edge of the bluff.

The line went tight, and Hunter's weight carried him forward. He slid down the line like an acrobat, straight toward the open window.

But he misjudged both his speed and the distance. Before he could brace himself, he slammed hard into the stone wall, just above the window.

Hunter grunted and almost lost his grip. His right hand slipped off the line, but he managed to cling tightly with his left. He looked down. This was one of the places where the castle melded with the cliff face. There was no battlement to land on if he let go. The chasm yawned greedily below him. Even in his armor, Hunter knew he'd never survive the fall.

As he hung above the abyss, Shadow mind-talked a warning. "The guard in the castle heard you! He's turned around and is coming back to look!"

Hunter grabbed the line with his free hand and held tight. "What about the one on the parapet?" he thought back. He glanced below and to his left, where the parapet stopped at the edge of the outer wall.

"He kept going," Shadow replied. "I think I might be able to sleep dart the one in the castle, but it'll be a tough shot into the wind—and there's a chance I might hit you, too."

An image of the chasm below flashed through Hunter's mind. "We don't want that!" he replied. "Hang tight and let me try something."

"Hang tight?"

"Don't do anything unless you have to," Hunter explained.

As the guard approached, Hunter drew his legs up, so that no part of him would be visible out the castle window. Even above the wail of the wind, he could hear the scrape of the Insector's chitinous feet over the corridor flagstones as the bug approached.

Hunter held his breath and tried to remain perfectly still.

The roachlike Insector poked his head out the window. He looked both left and right, then peered down the cliff face.

Hunter clung desperately to the line just over the Insector's head. His hands and arms felt as though they were on fire from the strain. Sweat beaded within his armor.

Seeing nothing, the Insector pulled his head back inside.

"He's gone!" Shadow gasped a moment later.

"So soon?" Hunter replied. "And I was having such a great time hanging out!" He lowered his legs and scrambled through the window into the castle.

Aqune threw open the doors to Mantid's grand meeting chamber and strode in. Dungobeet trailed behind her, pausing cautiously in the doorway.

From his throne at the opposite end of the room, Mantid looked at the young warrior appraisingly.

"Well," he asked, "have you assembled your forces?"

"I don't know how things usually work around here," Aqune said, glancing at Beerain, Buguese, and Grasshop, who were seated to one side, "but when I say I'll do something, I do it." She smiled and bowed mockingly to the others.

Grasshop and Beerain rose, anger flashing across their inhuman features. Buguese put a hand on each of their shoulders. After a moment, they sat back down.

Mantid glanced from his Insector lieutenants to the human girl. Slowly, he inclined his monstrous head in an approving nod. A low chuckle rumbled through his armored form.

"I've brought enough firefly warriors and mecha-spiders to tear down the walls of Arachnia stone by stone," Aqune boasted.

"Show me," Mantid said, rising and crossing to her.

Aqune went to a set of crystal doors set into one wall of the audience chamber. She opened the doors and said, "After you." She gestured to the balcony beyond.

Mantid went outside and Aqune followed. The balcony overlooked the long, winding road that led up the mountain slope to the Insector tyrant's castle. The road was black with mecha-spiders and their Insector riders.

Mantid nodded approvingly.

"My mecha-spiders are immune to stun blasts and most other Spider Rider weapons," she said. "Sleep darts merely bounce off their metal skins. My mecha do not eat, they do not sleep, they do not grow tired. As I've told you, each is equipped with a variety of weapons as well as grapples for climbing the walls of Arachnia. Their operators are expertly trained. Are the new lightning throwers you promised ready for me?"

"They are," Mantid replied, "though we will not be using them on Arachnia."

"What?" Aqune asked. "Why not?"

"Our objective has changed," Mantid replied.

Anger flashed across Aqune's angular face, and her eyes narrowed. "What do you mean?" she asked.

Mantid smiled. "Why go to the Spider Riders when, even at this moment, they are coming to us? Prince Lumen has foolishly marched his army out of Arachnia. He is coming in force to attack my fortress, even as we speak."

"Why?" Aqune asked.

"Because I have something he wants," Mantid replied.

Aqune nodded knowingly. "The shard," she said. "I heard a rumor you crippled their Oracle. Does Lumen have any idea that I have allied with you?"

"None at all," Mantid said.

A wicked smile creased the former Spider Rider's face. "Then we have him!" she said.

"Yes," said Mantid. "You will conceal your mecha in the mountains along the route to my fortress. My remaining Big Four Insectors will march my army out to meet the foolish prince head-on. As we engage him in battle, your forces will sweep down, unexpected, and destroy them."

Aqune nodded appreciatively. "Then this is the end of the Spider Riders!"

24
In the Maze of Mantid

Hunter crept carefully through the winding corridors of Mantid's castle. He'd changed into pedestrian mode, so there would be no chance of his armor clanking on the flagstones and giving him away. He hoped stealth would make fighting unnecessary—at least until he found the shard.

Soon, though, all the corridors began to look alike to him, and he realized he had no idea where he was going. Rather than sneak around until someone caught him, he decided to chance some mind talk.

"Shadow," he thought, "do you have any idea where the shard might be? It's like a maze down here."

No reply. Dead silence.

A knot formed in Hunter's stomach.

"Shadow?"

He pressed back into a doorway as, barely twenty feet away, a huge swarm of Insectors marched down a hallway at the end of the corridor. Every one of the cockroaches was fully armed.

Hunter swallowed hard, grateful they hadn't seen him.

A voice appeared in his mind—not the gruff, male voice of his spidery companion, but the gentle tones of the Oracle.

"Follow them," she said.

"Follow them where?" he thought back, but already the presence had faded.

As quickly as he could, Hunter sneaked after the long line of Insector warriors and followed them down into the castle. As he did, an image of a map began to form in his mind. Though he couldn't hear her, he knew the Oracle was still with him.

If only she could tell him more! But she probably didn't dare risk using strong telepathy so close to the enemy.

Finally, the cockroaches marched through a huge doorway and joined a throng of warriors already in the room. Hunter stopped at the edge of the huge doorway and pressed himself against the wall, out of sight. The room must have been deep within the castle, for a river of fiery lava flowed through it. The room was alive with activity as Insectors hoisted huge vats of molten iron out of the blazing river. They poured the flaming metal into molds to make weapons—enough to equip a vast Insector army. Sparks filled the air; the heat of the room was oppressive.

A horde of Insectors was massing on the far side of the chamber, next to a wide passageway leading downward. Unarmed cockroach warriors took up the new weapons and prepared themselves for battle.

Hunter shuddered. This must be part of the force that Mantid was sending to meet the other Spider Riders. These Insectors were hoping to kill Hunter's friends!

Near the wide passageway on the far side of the room stood two completed lightning throwers, waiting to deal death to the Turandot and destroy their proud city.

The sight of the swarming monsters and their deadly weapons made Hunter's skin crawl. He pressed himself back against the wall next to the entrance as two roach warriors passed within ten feet of him.

"If only I could bring this whole rotten hive down around their heads!" he thought.

Then Hunter felt the Oracle's presence strongly again. "Remember your mission. The passage across the chamber," she said. As she spoke, the map forming in his mind became clearer. Now he knew where the shard was and where he had to go. "Providence shall smile upon you, my child," the Oracle said. Then her presence faded away.

Hunter took a deep breath to steady his nerves. He had to cross the Insector-filled chamber to reach the passage. He wished that Sparkle were with him so he could share her invisibility power once more.

But she wasn't. With any luck, she was safely on her way back to Arachnia. Maybe next time Hunter went to the Forge, he could add that power to his manacle as well. Being invisible would definitely come in handy right now.

Then something occurred to him. Every time the Insectors poured liquid metal into a mold, the whole room filled with sparks, smoke, and steam. If he timed it just right, he could make it to the passageway without being seen.

Hunter waited and, during the next pour, took his chance.

He dashed across the room, through the billowing steam and smoke. The passageway opened before him, and he ran inside, undetected.

The tunnel angled down, farther into the volcanic mountain. Once Hunter had gone a few dozen yards, the light from the lava pit died away.

His fingers played across the surface of his manacle, activating a built-in glow light. Its soft, greenish shine gave him enough light to see but not enough, he hoped, to give him away to Mantid's guards.

Hunter moved carefully, following the map in his memory and listening for Insectors. Torchlight glowed ahead of him, so he switched off his manacle light.

Keeping to the shadows, he discovered two roach warriors standing guard beside a huge, heavy metal door. In his mind, Hunter saw a picture of the final shard. It was in the room beyond the door.

Hunter drew his stun sword and leaped out of the passageway. He slashed twice and felled the guards before they even knew what was happening. He paused just long enough to twist off their life force medallions and stuff them into his belt. Now only the metal door lay between him and his objective.

"Arachna might!" he whispered, calling on the power of his manacle. Instantly, his armor formed around him.

Hunter Steele smiled. With the room buried so deep in the castle, and with so much activity in the foundry room nearby, there was little chance that anyone would hear what he planned to do next.

He stepped back, took aim, and activated his sonic charge. The weapon crumbled the rock wall and vibrated the door off its massive hinges.

Hunter stepped through the opening.

The final shard lay atop a pedestal shaped like a swarm of insect claws. Hunter looked around, using the enhanced sensory apparatus in his manacle to scan the room. There were no apparent traps, but it all felt too easy to him.

He touched a few symbols on his manacle and played out a grappling line. The line terminated in a small metal spider, whose legs had been designed for gripping.

With a flick of his wrist, he snapped the line toward the shard. The metal spider hit the crystal's surface and latched on.

Hunter yanked the line and caught the shard as it flew back to him. The claws of the pedestal snapped shut on the empty air where the shard had been. Greenish venom dripped from the claws and spattered on the floor.

Hunter smiled, tucked the shard into a compartment in the belt of his armor, and ran back the way he'd come. He fed power from his manacle into the armor, increasing his speed as he went.

He dashed through the armory during another cloud of sparks and steam. "I need to get out of the castle fast, before anyone catches me," he thought.

Hunter was cautious as he ran but apparently not cautious enough. Alarms clanged as he sprinted through the twisting corridors and up the castle's winding stairways.

"Either they spotted me or they've discovered the shard missing," Hunter thought. "It doesn't matter which."

Dodging Mantid's patrols, he eventually reached the same window by which he'd entered. As he did, the guard patrolling that corridor spotted him. The cockroach ran toward Hunter, brandishing its curved spear.

Hunter pointed at the Insector and said, "Stun blast!" Energy burst from Hunter's manacle. The bug warrior flew across the corridor, crashed into a wall, and slumped to the floor, unconscious.

Hunter climbed the windowsill, jumped up, and grabbed the line he'd slid down on.

"Shadow!" he thought. "Be ready to run! I've got the shard, but the whole fortress is after me!"

As quickly as he could, Hunter climbed hand-over-hand up the slender line toward where he'd last seen his arachnid friend.

Roach warriors appeared on the parapet and spotted him. They shouted curses and shot arrows in Hunter's direction.

"Shadow, could you sleep dart those guys?" Hunter called, neither pausing nor looking back. Thunder crashed around him, and lightning lit the mountain peak ahead.

Shadow didn't reply. Had mind talk been shut down again?

Hunter concentrated hard, trying to contact the Oracle, but without any luck.

An arrow struck his thigh, but his armor stopped it.

"Shadow!" he thought. "I could really use some help here!"

As he neared the mountainside the roaches finally got smart. They stopped shooting at Hunter and, instead, crept up the castle wall to cut his line.

"Shadow!" Hunter thought…but too late!

With a slash of a crooked dagger, one of the roaches severed Hunter's lifeline.

The rope went slack. Hunter swung through the air and smashed into the face of the bluff.

He grunted in pain but managed to keep his grip on the line. "Shadow!" he shouted aloud.

Again, no reply.

The ledge lay only a few yards above him. Using what remained of the web line, Hunter quickly scaled it.

Anger boiled in his blood as he reached the top. "Shadow," he snapped, "what's the matter with—"

Then he froze.

At the top of the cliff face lay Shadow, stiff and unmoving.

25
Quest's End

Hunter stared at the spider for several long moments, unable to believe his eyes. Shadow lay on his back, his long legs curled inward in a death grasp. His exoskeleton looked gray and pale, not black and shiny as it usually did. Even the hairs on his mighty carapace looked stiff and brittle.

"Shadow!" Hunter cried desperately. At the same time, he put every ounce of energy that he possessed into trying to establish a mind link.

Nothing.

Hunter touched the spider's carcass. It seemed very cold, even for a spider. He tried to shake Shadow, but the spider didn't budge at all. His immense bulk lay unmoving, lifeless.

"Shadow!" Hunter cried.

He sank to his knees and wept. The clouds swirling overhead burst, and pelting rain splashed down around them. Hunter didn't care.

"Shadow!" he thought, but no reply came.

Hunter wiped the tears from his eyes. "I should have listened when you said you felt sick," he told the lifeless spider. "I should have listened to you when you said you didn't like water! That's when the trouble began, after we swam to Quagmiro. Something in that awful swamp water must have poisoned you!"

Hunter laid his head on his friend's body. "If only I hadn't brought you to this terrible place!" he said. "Then maybe the arachnid doctors could have cured you!"

The stinging rain pelted his face, but Hunter didn't care. His best friend in the whole Inner World was dead! What did anything else matter?

Then he remembered. Other things *did* matter: the shard! Hunter staggered to his feet once more. He gazed off, down the mountainside, the way he and Shadow had come. The trip back would be more difficult without the spider, but Hunter had to make it. He had to return the shard to Arachnia.

Then he saw something glimmering through the valleys between the mountain peaks. A remote flash of lightning played off gleaming metal. Hunter called up his distance viewer and peered at the faraway glittering objects. In a mountain pass beyond Mantid's fortress, a thousand metal spiders had gathered, poised to strike like two great silver pinchers.

Hunter knew the Spider Riders would be coming through that pass, intending to decoy the Insector army away from Mantid's palace so Hunter could escape with the shard. But the brave riders had no idea that an army of deadly robot spiders was waiting in ambush! He had to warn his friends.

Hunter patted Shadow's unmoving head. "I'm sorry," he whispered to the dead spider. "I don't want to leave you here for the Insectors to find, but I don't really have any choice. Corona and the others need us...need *me*."

Hunter turned and ran down slope as fast as he dared. "Good-bye, old friend!" he called, without looking back. "Good-bye, Shadow!"

The words nearly turned to a sob, but he blinked back the tears and focused on his mission. Hunter knew he had to warn the others, but he also needed to get the shard back to the city. With Shadow, he might have managed, but alone...?

"How can I do both?" he wondered desperately.

Then it occurred to him: mind talk. He could try to use mind talk to contact the other spiders and their riders.

He skidded over the slick rocks of the mountainside, trying to mentally call his friends. "Corona! Venus! Igneous! Lumen!" he thought. "Look out! The Insectors have set a trap! An army of robot spiders is going to ambush you! Watch out! Shadow is dead! I have the shard, but I don't know if I'll get to the city in time for the Oracle to help!"

The desperate thoughts echoed in Hunter's brain, but no reply came. He had no way of knowing if anyone had heard him.

He kept concentrating, kept trying to send the message, kept trying not to think about how much easier this would be with Shadow to help him. If he thought about the spider too much, he would just break down in tears again, and he didn't have time for that.

"Corona!" he thought, but as he did, his foot slipped on a rain-slick stone.

Hunter fell hard onto his back. The muddy slope beneath him gave way. He skidded downhill, banging into projecting rocks as he went. He tried to stop himself, but his fingers just skidded off the wet rocks. It was like when he'd fallen into the Inner World, so many weeks before.

As he slid, lightning crackled overhead. Through the rain, Hunter thought he saw flying shapes silhouetted against the sky. Were the Insectors looking for him? "I never should have spent so much time mourning over Shadow's body!" he thought.

He stopped with a sudden thud at the bottom of a craggy ravine. His armor had kept him from being injured, but he still felt battered and bruised.

With a pained grunt, Hunter lifted himself out of the mud. He glanced at his manacle, checking the compass that always pointed toward the Arachnian plateau.

It pointed up the ravine and to his right—nearly back the way he'd fallen. He cursed himself for being an idiot and began climbing.

A rock outcrop projected from the mountainside ahead of him. Hunter called up his spider grapple and threw it. The tiny metal insect latched on, and Hunter pulled himself up.

"That's easier than it could have been," he thought. He leaned against the rock and took a deep breath.

As he did, lightning flashed, revealing a dozen or more hulking forms standing just ahead of him. They completely blocked the small valley into which he'd climbed.

"Cockroach warriors!" Hunter realized.

In the midst of the enemy stood something that Hunter had never seen before, a towering humanoid shape with an armored face like that of a giant praying mantis. Purple robes trimmed with gold draped the monster's titanic form.

Hunter gasped—this creature had to be Mantid.

The creature smiled malevolently. "So," it said, its voice a deadly purr, "this is the boy who dared steal my shard. Return it to me, and I *may* let you live."

"No way!" Hunter said.

Mantid cocked his head in a very insectlike manner. "You're brave and cunning," the tyrant said, "like the girl

Aqune, the leader of the robot spiders. She was a Spider Rider once, just like you. Perhaps you could become my ally, as she has."

A cold chill ran down Hunter's spine. So, this Aqune, the leader of the robot spiders, was a Turandot—a human, like him—and she had joined forces with the Insectors!

Mantid held out one terrible clawed hand toward Hunter. "Well?" the Insector asked. "What are you waiting for? Hand it over!"

Hunter gritted his teeth. "I'd rather eat hot lava," he replied.

"Very well," Mantid said. He glanced at his roach warriors. A sharp command burst from his inhuman lips. "Kill him!"

26
Hunter vs. Mantid

In the mountains near Mantid's fortress, a faint cry echoed over the mind link that Princess Sparkle shared with her spider, Hotarla.

"Was that Hunter?" Sparkle asked.

"You expect me to know?" the spider replied. "I'm so tired I can hardly move."

"Well then, stop moving and listen!"

Hotarla stopped. For several reasons the two hadn't gone very far since leaving Hunter. One was that Sparkle didn't really want to leave, no matter what the Oracle had said. Another was that Hotarla was exhausted from their days of difficult travel. The spider moved very slowly and needed frequent rests. The third reason also had to do with the spider's exhaustion. To make the going less painful, Hotarla had chosen the easiest paths, rather than the quicker ones Hunter had followed.

After all they'd been through since leaving the city, Hotarla was more than happy to stop again. She and Sparkle concentrated, listening to the mind link.

"Yes!" Sparkle cried. "I hear him!"

"I don't," Hotarla said.

"Well, I'm a princess," Sparkle replied. "Powerful mind talk runs in my family."

She concentrated again for a moment. "Hunter's in trouble," she finally said. "He needs our help!"

"He told us to go home," Hotarla reminded her. "He *ordered* us to go home."

"He can't give us orders," the princess said haughtily. "Besides, when he told us to go home, he didn't know he'd get in trouble. Come on! We have to find him."

"Princess, we really shouldn't—"

"Who's in charge here?" Sparkle asked. "Let's go."

Reluctantly, the small battle spider picked herself up and headed back in the direction where they'd left Hunter.

"You've been gaining weight again," the spider said.

"Not since we started this mission!" Sparkle replied.

"No," Hotarla said, "but recently."

The princess rolled her eyes. "Of course I have," she said. "I'm growing up. And you are, too. The more missions we go on, the stronger you'll get and the easier it will be to carry me."

They backtracked as quickly as they could, the princess urging the spider on whenever Hotarla got weary—which was very often.

Soon they came to the cliffside where they'd parted company with Hunter and Shadow.

"I don't see him," Sparkle said. "Do you?"

"No," Hotarla replied. "But there are signs that they climbed up the rocks here."

"Maybe to get a better vantage point," Sparkle suggested.

"Maybe," Hotarla agreed.

At the princess's urging, the spider climbed up the rain-slick rock face. The going was tricky, but they soon reached the second ledge overlooking the castle.

As they did, they both froze.

There, lying upturned in a puddle of rain was the body of Shadow.

Sparkle gasped. "Oh, Hotarla!" she cried. "Shadow's dead! Is Hunter...?"

"I don't see his body," the spider replied.

"Could the Insectors have taken him prisoner?" Sparkle asked.

"If they did, we'll never see him again," Hotarla said.

"Don't think that way!" Sparkle cried. She got off the spider's back and knelt down in the mud next to Shadow.

She laid a hand on the big spider's unmoving head. "Oh! What do you think happened to him?" Tears streamed down her face, and she didn't bother to wipe them away.

Thunder shook the mountainside, making Sparkle jump.

"What is it?" Hotarla asked, fear in her voice. "Is it the lightning?"

"N-no!" Sparkle said. "S-something moved! Something moved inside Shadow's body!"

Shadow's carapace began to shake and split open.

Sparkle and Hotarla watched, awestruck, unable to tear their eyes away from the terrible sight.

"My prince," Igneous said, "our scouts report Mantid's forces heading straight down the valley in our direction." The Spider Rider captain-general smiled. "It seems the villain may have emptied his entire castle to fight us."

Lumen swallowed hard and then nodded. "Good," he said. "That will give Hunter a better chance to recover the shard—and maybe we can pick off some Insector leaders at the same time."

"The scouts indicate that the remaining Big Four are riding among the Insector troops," Igneous said.

"Are any of them airborne?" Lumen asked.

"Not as yet," Igneous replied. "It may be the storm is keeping them grounded. They seem to be mostly roaches."

"Yes," Lumen said, "only Mantid's elite roaches fly well in the rain. That's a break for us."

Igneous smiled again. "We could hardly have planned it better."

Lumen concentrated on using mind talk so the whole Spider Rider force could hear him. "The Insectors are riding out to meet us," he said. "Corona, as soon as we get through the pass, your legion will ride with me. Igneous's riders will circle to the left. We'll catch the enemy in a pincer movement and crush them."

Riding nearby, Corona nodded her understanding. "Yes, my prince. Any word from Hunter yet?" This last thought she shielded from everyone but Lumen, Igneous, and Magma.

"None," Lumen replied.

"If the Earthen doesn't get the shard," Igneous put in, "we'll be fighting the whole of Mantid's troops for nothing."

"Not for nothing," Magma said, joining the mind link. "Taking down a bunch of Insectors is a good enough reason to fight, so far as I'm concerned."

"If Hunter fails," Lumen thought, "we'll just have to take the shard the old-fashioned way—by storming Mantid's fortress."

Then, he opened the mind link to all the troops again. "Ready?" he cried. "Let's go! For Arachnia! For the Oracle!"

The hills shook with the Spider Riders' reply.

"HIZZ-AHHH!"

High in the hills, Aqune watched as a small force of Spider Riders split off from the main group.

She smiled, remembering the tactic from the days she herself had been a rider.

No matter how often the Spider Riders used this ploy, the Insectors never seemed to catch on. Bug-size brains, she supposed.

This time would be different, though. This time there would be no great Spider Rider victory.

Soon, she and her forces would spring from concealment, trapping the hated Spider Riders between her machines and the main bug force.

Then haughty Prince Lumen and proud Igneous and all the rest would die.

"Sorry, I don't feel like dying today!" Hunter Steele said. He raised his manacle, pointed it at the advancing Insectors and called, "Sonic charge!"

Quick as lightning, Mantid crossed his scythelike arms in front of his armored body. As he did, the air around the Insector warriors shimmered.

Hunter's sonic charge blasted forth, but it stopped short of his enemies, cascading around them like waves breaking against a rocky shore. Mantid laughed.

A chill ran down Hunter's spine. "Mantid protected them with some kind of energy shield," he thought. "Can he protect them while they're fighting me?"

Hunter drew his sword as the roach warriors rushed him. They brandished sawtooth spears, four charging at once.

*

195

"If I keep my back to the gulley," Hunter thought, "they can't rush me from that side. Not unless they can fly in this rain."

He parried two of the spears and stepped away from the third. The fourth hit him in the left thigh, but his armor turned aside the point, which did him no harm.

Hunter slashed high at one roach's face. When it parried, he whipped his sword in the opposite direction, catching the roach's partner in the throat.

The second roach gasped and fell to the muddy ground, stunned.

Hunter smiled.

Another roach rushed forward to take its fallen comrade's place.

Mantid watched the scene with cool detachment. "What's so special about you?" he asked Hunter mockingly. "You're just another weak human boy!"

"That's what you think, bug face!" Hunter replied. He ducked under the thrust of another spear and ran his sword through the Insector carrying it.

As he pulled the blade out, though, a second roach clouted him on the back of his neck with a spear shaft.

Hunter's armor kept the blow from killing him, but spots still burst behind his eyes. He staggered and two more rushed in, stabbing with their spears.

Again Hunter's armor stopped potentially deadly blows. He fell face first in the mud, barely keeping his grip on his sword.

"Honestly," Mantid said, "I don't know what the Oracle sees in you creatures. So soft...so weak..."

"The Oracle!" Hunter thought. "Why am I wasting time here? I need to help her! I need to help my friends!"

Hunter concentrated, channeling power from his manacle into his armor. As the roaches stabbed at him, he pushed up hard with his arms and legs.

He sprang into the air like a leaping spider.

"Sonic charge!" he called as he sailed over the attacking roaches.

This time, Mantid was not among the roach warriors to protect them. Hunter's blast pounded six of them into the mud. They lay there, twitching.

Hunter leaped again, putting manacle energy into his legs this time. He bounded high into the air, over the rest of the roaches and past Mantid.

He hit the ground beyond the villains and began running downhill once more. He hated to run away from a fight, but reaching his friends with the shard was far more important.

Suddenly, though, searing pain lanced through his back.

The force of the blow spun Hunter around, and he saw Mantid standing ten yards behind him.

One of the Insector tyrant's claws smoldered with evil energy. Mantid smiled.

Hunter staggered to his feet.

The roach warriors leaped toward him. They couldn't fly effectively in the rain, but they could use their wings to imitate Hunter's prodigious jumps.

They bounded forward as Hunter struggled to raise his sword one final time.

27
A Hero Reborn

Hunter parried the roach warriors' first spear, and then the second.

He'd lost the advantage of fighting with his back to the gully, though. Using their wings to aid their leaps, the elite roaches soared through the rain and over his head, quickly surrounding him.

Hunter knew his armor, strong as it was, couldn't stand up to repeated Insector beatings. Though only nine of the monsters remained, that was more than enough to finish him off. And even if Hunter could defeat them, he'd still have to deal with Mantid.

Cold sweat broke out on Hunter's forehead. His power manacle blinked weakly, nearly depleted of energy. "I can take out one or two," he thought, "but not all of them."

He turned from one roach to the other, trying to anticipate where the final, deadly attack might come from.

"The Oracle said I wouldn't die in Mantid's castle," Hunter thought grimly, "but she didn't say anything about dying in the mountains *outside* the castle!"

As if reading his thoughts, Mantid laughed.

One of the roaches rushed forward, aiming its spear for Hunter's gut. He stepped out of the way and smashed his left fist into the startled roach's face.

The big Insector went down, and Hunter cried, "Sonic charge!"

The howling blast took out two more before the manacle's energy gave out.

The remaining six roach warriors rushed him from all sides. Mantid just stood in place and laughed ruthlessly.

Hunter prepared to die.

As the Insectors came in on him, though, three of them suddenly staggered and fell face first into the mud. Small purple sleep darts protruded from the unconscious warriors' necks.

Hunter spun away from two of the spears trying to stick him. He parried the third roach's weapon with his sword and slashed back.

The roach parried in turn, but Hunter ducked away, and opened up some space between them. He could hardly believe his luck! They'd heard him! The Spider Riders had heard his call, and they'd come to his rescue!

He turned to see who his savior was, and his eyes nearly popped out of his head.

Bounding over the side of the valley came a huge, familiar black body.

"Shadow!" Hunter cried.

"It's good to see you, too," Shadow thought back.

"But—" Hunter began.

"Explanations later," the big spider said. "Fighting now." He landed next to Hunter, who quickly scrambled up onto his friend's back.

"Let's kick some Insector butt!" Hunter said. He glanced back at Mantid. Shadow's sudden appearance seemed to have surprised the Insector leader. Hunter smiled, glad for the lucky break.

Several of the roaches Hunter had stunned earlier had regained their senses. Eight of the warrior bugs now faced Hunter and his arachnid companion.

"As you might say," Shadow thought, "'piece of cake.'" He lunged forward, knocking down two of the roaches with his legs while Hunter felled a third.

"Watch out for the big guy," Hunter warned. "He's the dangerous one!"

Shadow ducked just in time as an energy blast from Mantid's claw seared over both their heads.

"Is that Mantid?" Shadow asked.

"I'm afraid so," Hunter replied. He parried the spear of a roach trying to skewer them and knocked the Insector back, over the edge of the ravine.

Shadow cast a capture web in Mantid's direction, but the Insector tyrant brought up his force shield once more. The web hit it and slid harmlessly to the soggy ground.

"Energy blasts, shields…" thought Shadow. "What else can he do?"

"I don't know," Hunter replied. "And I really don't want to find out." As he thought it, Hunter flattened another roach while Shadow webbed the remaining three. Now only Mantid remained.

"We can take him," Shadow thought. "He doesn't look so tough." He angled toward the Insector leader, looking to pounce.

A sudden screeching noise, louder than any thunder, filled the air. The blast sent Shadow and Hunter reeling head over heels. Only their armors' automatic ear protectors kept them from being knocked out.

They crashed hard into a boulder.

"Ouch!" Shadow thought. "I felt that—even through my new armor."

"A s-sonic charge!" Hunter thought back, trying to clear his head. "He has a sonic charge!"

The big black spider staggered, trying to regain his feet. The whole world seemed to be swimming around them.

Mantid moved through the storm toward them, his purple robes billowing around his hideous form. He raised one glowing, scythelike claw. A smile cracked his monstrous face.

"Now," he said, "I will take back my shard."

As Mantid spoke, though, a small capture web streaked through the air toward him.

Mantid looked up, startled, and managed to fend the webbing off with his glowing forearm. The web sizzled and dripped over his buglike face.

"Argh!" he cried as hot, sticky goo dripped onto his eyes.

The tyrant backed away from Hunter and Shadow as Sparkle and Hotarla crested a nearby rise.

"Keep away from them, you mean old monster!" Sparkle cried. She and her spider looked wet and bedraggled, but angry fire burned within their eyes.

"Sparkle! Hotarla!" said Hunter. "Am I glad to see you!"

"Me, too," the princess replied via mind talk. "Let's get him!"

Using their telepathy to coordinate their moves, Shadow and Hotarla spread out so Mantid couldn't target both of them at once.

"Now!" Shadow thought. He and Hotarla fired a volley of sleep darts at their enemy.

Mantid's scythelike claws flashed through the lightning-dappled gloom, knocking the darts out of the air before they could hit him.

He gazed coldly from Hunter to Sparkle then leaped into the air.

Instinctively, the Spider Riders brought up their weapons, but Mantid spread his wings and arced away from them, back toward his fortress.

"We beat him!" Sparkle yelled.

"Yeah," Hunter said, "at least for the moment. Let's get out of here while we still can."

"Do you have the shard?" the princess asked.

Hunter nodded, and the four of them turned and hurried down the mountainside as fast as they were able.

"Do you know if the others got my message?" Hunter asked as they rode.

"What message?" Sparkle asked. "I heard something over the mind link, but I thought you just needed help. It wasn't a strong message, like my brother could do, but it was enough to get me looking for you."

"I heard the cry, too," Shadow said. "That's why I came out of my molting so soon. You're getting better at mind talk. Pretty soon you'll be as good as all the others—maybe better."

"Well, I wish I was good enough to get that warning to Lumen," Hunter thought back. "Could either you or Hotarla do it?"

"Not from this range," Shadow replied, "not in these conditions."

They kept hurrying across the rocky slopes, toward the valley where they knew the others were marching toward Mantid's fortress.

As they traveled, Hunter shared what he knew about the ambush and Aqune with Shadow, Hotarla, and Sparkle.

"Aqune!" Sparkle said, practically spitting the word.

"So you know her?" Hunter said.

"Everyone in Arachnia knows her—or, at least, knows of her," Sparkle replied. "She tried to kill my brother and take over the Spider Riders. She wants to be queen of Arachnia, but it'll never happen."

"So she's a real threat."

"If she has an army…" the princess began. She stopped and looked worried.

"We'll just have to get there in time to warn your brother and the rest," Hunter thought.

"I hope so," Sparkle said, "but Hotarla is getting very tired. This has been a tough journey for us, you know."

Hunter slapped his palm to his forehead. "What are we thinking?" he said. "You shouldn't be coming with me. You should be taking the shard back to the Oracle."

"No way!" Sparkle said, repeating a phrase she'd often heard from Hunter. "I'm not going to ride away from battle when my brother is in trouble."

"But you could get the shard to the Oracle," Hunter said. "Maybe she could help us."

"We'd never get there before that witch Aqune kills Lumen and the rest," Sparkle pointed out.

"She's right," Shadow said.

The princess puffed herself up. "Besides," she said, "I'm the princess. I should be giving *you* orders."

Hunter sighed. "Let's just go rescue everybody, okay?"

"Okay."

They kept moving as quickly as they could, though the rain made the mountainsides slick and treacherous. Hunter knew that Sparkle and Hotarla were nearly exhausted, but neither the princess nor her small spider complained.

"Any idea how far away we are?" Hunter thought to Shadow.

"It's hard to tell," the spider replied. "The storm, the terrain, and other factors can interfere with mind talk. I'm starting to hear murmurings, but I can't tell if they're over the next ridge or leagues away."

Hunter nodded, wishing they could get to the battlefield faster. "You said earlier that you had been molting," he said to Shadow. "Do you mean shedding your skin?"

"Yes," Shadow said. "Every ten years or so a battle spider's exoskeleton renews. My new armor is stronger than the old, and a bit larger, too."

"I noticed," Hunter said.

"The aching I was experiencing was a symptom of the molting—but I was so distracted that I didn't realize it," Shadow said. "By the time I realized what was going on, I was already transforming. When the change comes, I can't mindtalk effectively. I'm sorry I scared you. I'm sorry you thought I was dead."

Hunter smiled and patted the spider on the back. "Just don't do it again," he said.

"Not for ten years," Shadow replied.

They topped a jagged ridge on the mountainside and a long valley stretched out below them. Down its middle wound a road leading from the land of the Spider Riders toward Mantid's castle. Something huge writhed across the valley floor.

Lightning flashed, scattering the rain-spattered darkness and revealing an ocean of warriors, stretching as far as the eye could see. Insector fought Spider Rider. Battle spiders leaped among the enemy. Swords flashed, manacle weapons blazed, and antenna blasts wailed.

Hunter glanced at Sparkle. She looked scared.

"Take the shard to the Oracle," he said to her.

"No," she replied. "I want to help."

Hunter could see that he had no chance to change the princess's mind. "Okay," he said. "Let's go."

28
Spider vs. Mecha-Spider

Prince Lumen and the Lost Legion battled at the head of the column of advancing Spider Riders. They fought the Insectors with fierce determination. The prince and Ebony held the center of the Spider Rider line, while Corona and her legion conducted forays into the enemy forces.

Venus bounded through the cockroaches, spraying webs and firing sleep darts. Corona cut down the enemy using her lance and the occasional stun bolt. Crystal, Geode, and the other warriors followed her example. They wiped out any Insectors trying to outmaneuver Lumen's group and then returned to the main Spider Rider army.

With a cry of "Hizz-ahhh!" Igneous, Magma, and their troops swept down on the enemy flank. They'd circled through the nearby foothills to attack the Insectors from the side. It was a classic Spider Rider tactic, and it seemed to be working brilliantly.

None of those engaged in the battle saw what Hunter saw, though—the metal forces of Aqune hidden nearby, waiting to spring their trap. Hunter wouldn't have spotted Aqune either, save for a chance flash of lightning glinting off spider-shaped metal.

"Did you see them?" he asked Shadow and Sparkle as they bounded through the hills toward the battlefront.

"Yes," the spider replied. "I've never seen anything like them before."

Sparkle nodded. "I saw them, too," she said. Across the mental link, Hunter could feel the girl's fear. "What are they?" she asked.

"They're metal spiders," Hunter replied. "That's what I saw from the mountain."

"But how can that be possible?" Sparkle asked. "Metal doesn't move on its own!"

"They're robots, Mantid said—that is, machines," Hunter said. "In my world people make all kinds of moving machines out of metal. We ride in metal vehicles, for instance, and fly in airplanes, which are like big metal birds."

"We have to warn my brother!" Sparkle thought. "We should be close enough now, if he can hear us over the noise of the battle."

"We'll all try together," Hunter said.

Linking their thoughts, all four of them concentrated on a powerful mind-talk message.

"Lumen! Igneous! Aqune is hiding in the hills with an army! She's about to ambush all of you!"

As they sent the message, two powerful cracks of lightning shot through the Spider Rider ranks. These were no bolts from above, though. They came from twin lightning throwers within the Insector ranks.

"Did anyone get the message?" Hunter asked.

"There's no way to know unless someone replies," Shadow said. "Those big lightning bolts may have distracted them or disrupted what we were trying to say."

"We need to try again!" Sparkle said desperately.

"Too late!" Hotarla cried.

As the smaller spider spoke, Aqune's forces swarmed down from the foothills toward the rear of the Spider Rider ranks.

"Look out!" Hunter, Shadow, Sparkle, and Hotarla all thought at once.

The Spider Riders turned just as Aqune and her mecha-spiders crashed into them. The former rider and her mechanical monsters felled two of Lumen's warriors before anyone grasped what was happening.

As one, all the Spider Riders nearest the traitor turned. Their spiders fired a barrage of purple sleep darts, but the darts bounced harmlessly off the machines' metal bodies. The firefly warriors sitting on the mecha-spiders' backs directed the mechanical monsters to attack.

"Oh, no!" Sparkle cried. "Lumen, look out!"

The prince must have heard his sister, for he turned his head toward Aqune just as she fired a stun bolt at him. Lumen brought up his shield and dispersed the bolt's power, but the sudden appearance of the metal spiders had clearly shaken him. His mental orders reached every rider in the valley, including Hunter.

"Fall back! Form a defensive circle!"

The Spider Riders cast capture nets at Aqune's legion. The mecha-spiders easily slashed through them with their metal claws.

The Spider Riders did as they were told, forming into a circle, though this left them trapped between the Insectors and Aqune's terrible forces. The Spider Riders blasted at the mecha legion with their manacle weapons, but only the lightning lance power seemed to have any effect. Mecha-spiders hit by it shook violently and then collapsed, their firefly masters unconscious. Not enough of the Spider Riders had that particular power, though.

"Igneous!" Hunter thought. "Try to capture those lightning throwers! They can shock the riders on Aqune's metal spiders! Metal conducts electricity!"

Igneous's surprised voice echoed back within Hunter's head. "Earthen? Is that you?"

"Yes! We've come to help!"

"Me, too!" Sparkle added.

Hunter could feel Igneous bristling across the mind link. "You should be returning to Arachnia—if you completed your mission."

"We did," Hunter said. "But we couldn't leave you to be ambushed."

"Join the fight, then!" Igneous commanded. "Oracle knows we could use the help! Attack the rear of Aqune's forces. If we can break their line…" He didn't need to finish the thought.

Hunter, Shadow, Sparkle, and Hotarla raced behind Aqune's forces and attacked.

Sparkle shot a stun bolt at the mecha nearest her, but it had no effect on the metal spider. The firefly operator's hands played across the spines near the spider's head, and the machine whirled to face the girl.

Hunter crashed his lance into the side of the mecha nearest him. The blow didn't slay the creature, but it did knock the metal spider into another one. The two tangled their legs for a moment, until their firefly riders sorted them out.

Hunter's lance knocked one of the riders from its saddle. The other pressed a stud near the machine's head, and two metal tubes popped out of the spider's back.

"Blasters!" Hunter thought desperately. "Look out!"

Shadow didn't understand the meaning of the word, but the urgency of Hunter's thought rang clear. The spider leaped straight up as the mecha fired at it.

The energy blasts streaked under them and blew up the hillside beyond. Sparkle screamed.

"Web them!" Hunter thought. "The blasters can't fire if they're webbed!"

Shadow did as Hunter commanded. He sprayed a stream of webbing at both of the weapon barrels. The Insector rider yanked on the spines behind the mecha's head.

The machine twisted and cut one of the webs out of the air. The other got through, though, and clogged one blaster's barrel.

Hunter swung around to that side, angled his lance over the clogged weapon, and struck the firefly rider in the chest. The impact unseated the Insector and sent him crashing to the ground, unconscious. Without its rider, the machine also crashed into the muddy earth.

Sparkle screamed again, and Hunter turned to see Hotarla struggling in the grasp of one of the metal spiders. Beyond her, many Spider Riders faced similar problems. Their weapons were proving ineffective against the terrible machines.

Several riders lay unconscious. Many, like Sparkle, were caught in the grip of their deadly, unliving foes. Corona, Magma, and Lumen remained free, but Insectors and mecha were pressing in all around them.

Mind talk became chaotic, confused chatter. Even Igneous seemed at a loss for what to do. He'd reached the lightning throwers on the ridge, chased off Grasshop, and disabled the guards. But he couldn't figure out how to fire the weapons against Aqune's forces.

"Keep fighting!" he ordered.

"Keep fighting!" Lumen echoed from the valley below his captain.

Aqune laughed. The rain and lightning made her look demonic. Her metal spider leaped at Geode, who stood between her and the prince.

Geode tried to stop her, but she bowled him over. The young warrior and his spider, Coal, crashed into the mud and lay unmoving.

"We're losing!" Shadow thought desperately. "The Spider Riders are losing!"

29
The Earthen's Triumph

Aqune's mecha-spider stepped over the fallen bodies of Geode and Coal. Lumen was fighting a swarm of cockroach warriors and didn't see her coming. Sweat poured from the prince's face as he slashed at the Insectors with his stun sword.

Aqune smiled a wicked smile. She raised her lance and charged at Prince Lumen's unprotected back. "This time," she said, "I will not fail!"

Suddenly, Magma and Brutus bounded in front of her. The big Turandot used his lance to deflect hers, then swung toward her head.

Aqune ducked and her metal spider backed out of range. The renegade rider's eyes narrowed. "You!"

Magma nodded. "It's been a while, Aqune," he said. "I see you're still up to your old tricks."

"I would be," she said, "if you'd just get out of my way. Move aside and I won't kill you."

Magma's face broke into a daring smile. "You won't kill me, even if I don't move aside," he boasted.

"You think I won't?" she asked angrily.

"I think you *can't*."

"You mean nothing to me now."

"I know that," Magma said, "but you never could take me in a fair fight."

Aqune's eyes narrowed. "Who said anything about fighting fair?"

Hunter ducked as the mecha-spider nearest him tried to take his head off with a razor-sharp claw. Shadow grabbed the metal spider's leg in his mandibles and held tight.

The machine's rider yanked on the spines mounted on the mecha's back. The metal creature bucked hard and shook free from Shadow's grip.

"These metal beasts are tough!" Shadow thought.

Hunter's eyes narrowed as he watched the firefly rider direct his mount. "I know the secret!" Hunter suddenly thought. "I know how to defeat Aqune's warriors!"

The mecha-spider's blaster ports opened and fired a burst at Hunter and Shadow. The battle spider was expecting it, though, and leaped out of the way. The blasts streaked harmlessly beneath them.

"Well, don't keep it a secret from the rest of us!" Shadow said. He cast his web again, clogging one of the mecha's blasters.

"Connect me to the other riders," Hunter said. "Everyone needs to hear this."

"Right," Shadow replied.

"The metal spiders are machines!" Hunter said over the mind link. "They're not alive! You can't hurt them! Concentrate on the riders! Without the riders guiding them, the machines are useless! They can't think on their own like our spiders can!"

"I'll test that theory," Shadow said as he leaped out of the way of another burst of weapons fire. He aimed carefully and put a sleep dart into the neck of the firefly warrior shooting at them.

The firefly slumped forward, out cold. Its machine stopped suddenly, crashing into another mecha-spider. Both went down, and Shadow cast a web over them.

"It works!" Shadow thought.

The other Spider Riders immediately changed tactics. Corona, Crystal, Igneous, and the rest began targeting the riders. They used their manacle weapons, their swords, and their lances to attack the firefly riders. The battle spiders used their mandibles, their legs, and their sleep darts.

Aqune's mecha-spider army began to fall, but there were still far more Insectors than Spider Riders.

Sparkle and Hotarla remained caught in a mecha-spider's powerful grip. It was all Hotarla could do to avoid being blasted by the machine's weaponry.

Hunter and Shadow charged forward. The big spider land-ed behind Sparkle's attacker, and Hunter drove his lance into the firefly rider's back. The rider fell unconscious, and the machine went limp.

Sparkle and Hotarla shook free from the mecha's grip.

"Th-thank you!" Sparkle gasped.

"Target the riders," Hunter reminded her.

Sparkle nodded. "We understand." She looked scared but determined as she and Hotarla raced off to fight a band of Insectors.

"She'll be all right," Shadow said as they went.

"Let's try another tactic," Hunter thought back. "Wind your webbing around their legs."

"But they'll just cut them or step out of them," Shadow replied.

"Not if you wind them tight," Hunter said. "They're not living creatures. If we tangle their legs, it should be impossible for their operators to control them."

"Let's do it!" Shadow said.

He and Hunter raced toward a band of mecha-spiders trying to scale the ridge to attack Igneous, who was up to his armpits in Insectors. Shadow circled the machines, spinning webs as he went and dodging enemy fire.

As Hunter instructed, Shadow pulled the sticky strands as tight as he could. The metal spiders cut some of the webbing, but they couldn't keep up with the fast-moving battle spider.

The mecha operators couldn't cope with the web strands entangling the legs of their machines. The mecha-spiders staggered and then fell, further entangling one another as they went. Once the riders were down, Hunter and Shadow quickly knocked them out.

"Brilliant!" Hunter said. "Tell the others." His head ached from concentrating on all the mind talk he'd been doing.

"Already done," Shadow replied.

Immediately, the other Spider Riders added the new tactic to their battle plan. With their weaknesses known, the mecha army's advantages in battle quickly disappeared. They began to fall left and right under the well-coordinated attack from Lumen's and Igneous's riders.

The regular Insectors fared no better. With their lightning throwers captured and their metal allies in disarray, Mantid's cockroaches became frightened. Many of them dropped their weapons and fled back toward Mantid's fortress—despite the orders of Buguese, who had been leading them. Beerain joined Grasshop in fleeing the battlefield.

Hunter smiled. Then, a voice in his head said, "I understand the riders control the machines, but how do they do it?"

It was Magma's voice. Hunter looked across the battlefield and saw the big Turandot in pitched combat with Aqune. The traitorous former rider was giving the big mercenary all the trouble he could handle.

Aqune's skill with her mecha-spider was much greater than that of her firefly army. She dodged nimbly aside when Brutus tried to snare her machine's legs; her armor and shield neatly deflected Brutus's sleep darts and the stun bolts that Magma hurled at her.

Both warriors wore grim, determined expressions as they circled each other, trying to gain advantage or land a telling blow.

"The spines on the spider's neck that Aqune manipulates are really levers that control the machine's movements," Hunter said. He ducked a blast aimed in his direction and knocked a cockroach off a battle scorpion with his lance.

"Got it," Magma said. Even across the chaos of the battlefield, Hunter could see him smile.

"Hang on, Magma," Corona said, interrupting Hunter's mind talk, "we're coming!"

"Keep back!" Magma bellowed. "This one is mine."

He stabbed at Aqune with his lance, but it was only a feint. As she brought up her shield to fend it off, Magma threw a plasma blast across her mecha's control levers.

Aqune shrieked, barely getting her hands out of the way as the metal levers melted. Her spider lurched to a sudden halt.

Brutus flung a capture web at her, but Aqune rolled off the back of her crippled machine, and the web missed. She landed on her feet and drew her sword.

She slashed hard and, whether by luck or design, caught Brutus in one of the freshly healed places where the Water Strykers had wounded him. The big spider winced and reeled back. Aqune said, "Force ram!"

A force bolt blasted from her armored hands and caught Brutus on his underside. The big spider fell backward, nearly landing on top of Magma.

Aqune raised her sword and stepped toward the downed rider.

As she did, Corona and Venus bounded in, with Hunter and Shadow right behind.

Cursing, the Turandot traitor turned and ran. She dodged between fighting Insectors, downed mecha, and embattled Spider Riders, but she couldn't match the speed and agility of Venus and Shadow.

"We've got her!" Hunter thought to Corona.

"Not yet!" Corona replied. "Look!"

Before either of them could do anything, Buguese swooped out of the sky and carried Aqune into the air. The traitorous rider didn't seem too pleased, though she didn't resist her new ally's attempt to rescue her.

"This isn't over!" she screamed back at the Spider Riders.

Corona pointed and shouted, "Lightning lance!"

White energy blazed from her manacled hand, streaking through the sky toward Buguese and Aqune. But the former rider activated her shield and deflected the blast. A moment later, she and Buguese disappeared into the rain-dappled sky.

"Rats!" Hunter said.

"We'll get her another day," Corona said. "Come on. We need to make sure Magma and the others are okay—and there are still Insectors to fight, too."

"Not many of them," said a happy voice. It was Prince Lumen, looking tired but proud as he rode up to them on Ebony. "We'll be cocooning thousands. The Insector army is in full retreat. Buguese fleeing was the final straw."

"Buguese is no fool," Igneous said, joining the conversation via telepathy. "Should we pursue, my prince?"

Hunter and the rest stared after the fleeing Insectors. Mopping up the rabble would be little trouble, but Mantid and his fortress remained strong. If the prince's army pursued, more Spider Riders would surely be injured—or killed.

Hunter thought of how the impulsive Lumen had rushed into the Centipedian vault, heedless of the danger, just a short time ago.

He feared he already knew the prince's decision.

30
The Quest Fulfilled

Prince Lumen looked from his escaping foes to his valiant but battered Spider Riders. His eyes grew cold and stern.

Hunter held his breath, waiting to see if the prince would order the Spider Riders to their deaths.

"No," Lumen said. "Let them go. Battle was never our purpose today, not unless…" He paused and looked directly at Hunter. "Earthen, do you have the final shard?"

Hunter patted one of the compartments in his armor and nodded. "The shard is safe and sound," he said, trying not to seem too relieved.

"Then cocooning Mantid will have to wait for another day," Lumen said. "We'll get them all eventually. Now we need to get the shard safely home."

"Yes, my prince," Igneous said. He telepathically ordered the rest of the Spider Rider army to break off and form up for the return home.

Crystal rode up, looking angry and impatient. "We should go after them now!" she said. "We have the advantage! We should wipe every Insector from the face of the Inner World!"

"There will be plenty of other days to fight," Corona noted. "How's Geode?"

"He'll live," Crystal reported, "as will Coal. They'll have some nasty bruises, though."

"As will I," said Magma, joining them.

"All of us will," Lumen said. "But there will be plenty of time to recover, once the Oracle is restored."

Hotarla limped wearily toward the group, a tired and bruised Princess Sparkle wobbling on her back. "Does that mean we can go home now?" Sparkle asked.

The elation of their victory buoyed the riders' long march back to the city of Arachnia. Even the wounded laughed and joked along the way.

The Spider Rider casualties had been light, considering the scope of the battle. Many sported injuries, but thanks to Hunter's timely information about how to fight the mecha, few had been badly hurt, and no one was killed.

The triumphant Spider Riders dragged almost two thousand cocoons across the grassy plain. They stopped at the Cavern of Cocoons at the base of the Great Mountains to deposit their webbed captives. Then they skirted Lake Arachnia and headed for their distant plateau.

Jubilant Turandot citizens lined the roadways all the way from Lake Arachnia to the city. They cheered the Spider Riders and gave them gifts of cool water and freshly baked sweets.

King Arachna met the army at the top of the great citadel's outer wall and led them in a parade through the streets of the capital.

Hunter didn't need Spider Rider telepathy to tell that everyone in Arachnia felt enormously proud and excited.

"We did it!" he thought to Shadow. "We did it!"

"Thanks to you," the spider replied. "And we got our parade as well!"

Hunter blushed. "You, Sparkle, and Hotarla helped, too," he said. "I'd never have escaped Mantid if not for all of you."

When they reached the palace, Hunter, Corona, Magma, Igneous, Lumen, and Sparkle went inside with the king. The rest of the riders stayed outside, in the city, to tend their wounds and celebrate with their friends and families. The spiders gathered in their compound, happy for the victory but equally happy to rest.

Magma looked longingly at the crowd as the castle doors closed behind him.

"Don't worry," Corona joked. "You'll be joining them in celebration soon enough."

Magma laughed and nodded.

King Arachna embraced both his children. "I'm proud of you both," he said. Then, looking at Sparkle, he added, "Though *you* weren't to leave the castle grounds."

For a moment the king looked very stern, and Sparkle looked crestfallen. Prince Lumen stepped forward.

"Princess Sparkle did very well, Father," he said. "Even if she *did* break the rules."

"I'd never have recovered the shard without her," Hunter added.

King Arachna nodded, then smiled. "So I've heard," he said. "You'll make quite a Spider Rider someday, Sparkle."

"Someday?" she asked hopefully.

"Yes," said the king. "And perhaps that day is near."

"You mean it, Father?" Sparkle said, excited almost beyond words.

The king nodded. "You can begin the final phase of your training in a few sleeps. Now, though, we have important business to attend to."

Sparkle nodded, tears budding at the corners of her eyes. She and the others followed the king, winding down through the castle and into the Sacred Sepulcher of the Oracle. There, Prince Lumen placed the final shard into the Oracle's golden crown.

Immediately the eyes of the statue opened. A bright golden light surrounded her lovely form. The remaining cracks that marred her beautiful figure healed, and her eighth and final arm unfolded from her chest.

The Oracle opened her hands, and multicolored flames sprang up in her palms. The fires burned brightly and danced with all the colors of the rainbow.

Hunter couldn't help but smile. He looked at Corona and saw that she was beaming as well. In fact, everyone in the room looked happier than Hunter had ever seen them.

The Oracle herself looked immensely pleased, too. All traces of stiffness had disappeared, and she looked almost fully human—despite remaining a statue.

"My faithful Spider Riders," she said, her voice brimming with love and admiration, "you have done better than even I had hoped. I thank you. The entire kingdom thanks you."

The king, the prince and princess, and the Spider Riders all bowed their heads. It took a moment for Hunter to catch on, but he quickly did the same.

"Your service has been exemplary," the Oracle continued. "Now peace shall reign over Arachnia and all the Inner World."

Hunter wondered if that meant the Insectors would just surrender now, but he didn't say anything.

"Mantid and Aqune will not give up so easily," Shadow's voice said via mind talk.

222

Hunter smiled, glad to have the spider with him.

"You have done exceptionally, Hunter Steele," the Oracle said, snapping him out of his reverie. "I knew I chose well when I picked you. The first part of your destiny is fulfilled."

Hunter blushed. "Just trying to help out," he said. He noticed Igneous and Lumen frowning at him just a bit, but he didn't care. At the moment, he felt as if he was sitting on top of the world.

"However," the Oracle continued, "I know there is something else that concerns you. Go. See to it now, while I speak with the others. Corona may go as well."

"What...?" Hunter began, a bit confused. Then he remembered.

"And, Magma, my brave mercenary," the Oracle added, "you may join the celebration if you wish."

Magma merely grinned.

Hunter, Corona, and Magma ran from the chamber at top speed. Soon, the big Turandot split off, heading for the outside, while Hunter and Corona continued on.

The two of them darted through the twisting corridors of the royal palace and into the deepest vaults below the castle.

Hunter's heart pounded as he ran, as much from excitement and nervousness as from exertion. He skidded to a halt outside the door to the Hall of Heroes. Corona stopped beside him. She took his hand.

They walked into the great, dimly lit hall together, and went to the farthest chamber. There, they found Petra's cocoon, still lying on its bier. The cocoon rose and fell with steady, regular breathing. A golden glow—the power of the Oracle—surrounded the comatose Spider Rider.

223

Hunter and Corona walked forward, hardly able to believe what they were seeing. As the glow faded, Corona took out her energy knife and carefully cut the webbing away from Petra's face.

Slowly, sleepily, Petra opened her eyes and gazed up at Hunter and Corona. Her voice was dry and weak from her time in suspended animation.

"Did…did we win?" she asked.

Hunter and Corona glanced at each other. They knew Petra meant not the recent battle, but the fight for the city of Arachnia—the battle in which she'd fallen.

Corona nodded and brushed a tear from the corner of her eye. "Yes," she said. "Yes, we won."

"Several times, actually," Hunter added with a smile.

Petra smiled back. "Good," she said. "I knew we would."

Hunter squeezed Corona's hand.

The two of them cut away the rest of Petra's cocoon and helped her to sit up. She wobbled a bit at first and seemed more than happy to accept their help.

"Was I out long?" she asked them.

"Not long," Hunter replied.

"Ages," Corona said at the same time.

Petra laughed a quiet laugh. Hunter and Corona smiled and helped her to stand.

As they did, Crystal, Geode, and Granite, the other members of the Lost Legion, raced into the chamber. When they saw Petra on her feet, they all burst into cheers. They ran forward and clapped their recovered leader on the back.

"We knew you'd come back to us," Geode said.

"Things weren't the same without you," added Granite.

"Well, they were pretty much the same," Crystal said, "lots of fighting and Insector plots. But they'll be even better now that you're back."

"We've got celebrations to get to," Granite said.

"And you can help me put the new medallions in my trophy case," Hunter added. He smiled at Petra, and she smiled back.

"Have you defeated all the Insectors while I slept, Earthen?" she asked.

"Oh no," Corona replied with a laugh. "We left a few for you."

"More than a few," Geode said.

"The Big Four is now down to three," Crystal noted, smiling broadly at the Earthen boy.

Hunter felt himself blush. "We've gained some new enemies, though," he added. "Like Aqune."

"Is she back?" Petra asked. "And here I thought I might catch some rest!"

"No rest for any of us," Crystal said. "Not while Mantid is still out there."

Petra looked earnestly at her friends. "Mantid can wait," she said. "Right now, I could use something to eat. Is anybody else hungry? I feel like I haven't eaten in weeks!"

Hunter, Corona, and the members of the Lost Legion all laughed.

Side by side, all of them walked out of the Hall of Heroes and into the eternally burning orange sunshine of Arachnia.

Tedd Anasti and Patsy Cameron-Anasti

Tedd and Patsy met when Tedd was producing live-action children's shows for Walt Disney Studios and Patsy auditioned for a role in one of his episodes. They discovered a mutual love for quality children's entertainment and became writing partners. Their first show as a team was the Emmy Award–winning series *The Smurfs* for Hanna-Barbera.

Over the next two decades, Tedd and Patsy wrote and produced more than 500 half hours of such children's television hits as Disney's *Timon and Pumbaa*, *Duck Tales*, and *The Little Mermaid*. They also wrote and produced the *Free Willy* television series for Warner Brothers and received their second Emmy Award for Tim Burton's *Beetlejuice*. Tedd and Patsy have received eight Emmy nominations, three Humanitas Prize nominations, the Governor's Media Award, and the Silver Angel Award for Excellence in Children's Television.

Tedd and Patsy have two children, Emily Rose and Teddy. It was their son's passion for spiders that inspired *Spider Riders*.

One day, Teddy, then only five, announced that he had captured ten black widows in their backyard in California. At first, Tedd and Patsy didn't believe their son had really captured black widows, but upon inspection found that it was true!

In order to get the boy to turn his deadly black widows in to the local nature center, Tedd and Patsy agreed to buy Teddy two nonpoisonous tarantulas—one male, one female. The Anasti household is now a tarantula breeding ground!

The Spider Boy, as he is known, became a hero to the

other kids in the neighborhood. Upon seeing how fascinated children are with spiders, Tedd and Patsy were inspired to write the novel *Spider Riders*—the story of a boy lost in a primitive underground world of warring giant insects where his best friend is a ten-foot battle spider.

Books in the Spider Riders Series

Spider Riders Book One: The Shards of the Oracle introduces the kingdom of Arachnia, in the Inner World, where a never-ending battle rages between a human race called the Turandot and a giant insect race called the Insectors. Defending the Turandot are the Spider Riders, fierce young warriors with special weapons who ride armored spiders ten feet tall. When Hunter Steele spirals down into the Inner World by mistake, he can't return home until he earns the right to become a Spider Rider himself. Then he must join them in their greatest challenge: recovering the stolen shards of their guardian power, the Oracle, from the evil mastermind who wants to rule the Inner World.
224 pp 5 ³⁄₁₆" x 7 ⅜" 1-55704-652-2 $5.99

• • • •

Spider Riders Book Two: Quest of the Earthen follows Hunter Steele as the Spider Riders go after Mantid—the merciless leader of the Insectors—and Mantid's new allies, Fungus Brain and Aqune. Only then can Hunter undertake the most dangerous mission alone—to penetrate the heart of Mantid's mighty fortress and prove himself a full-fledged Spider Rider.
240 pp 5 ³⁄₁₆" x 7 ⅜" 1-55704-681-6 $5.99

The Spider Riders books are written by Tedd Anasti and Patsy Cameron-Anasti, with Stephen D. Sullivan.
